HE WAS BREAKING OPEN A TOMB . . .

. . . feeling around in the cavity. There was a great deal of dust, then he touched what he had been hoping to find . . . a bone.

It was a thigh bone. He moved his fingers along it to the hip bone, the ribs, the jaw bone, the teeth. He felt around, the dome of the forehead, the eye holes, dry. He pulled out the skull, the whole of the skull and felt it in the dark, felt the brittleness of the bone.

He was with death, but somehow for him this death was now his friend. He raised the skull to his forehead, pressed the dome against his brow. The hiss sounded far off, but it was there, very faint, very faint. It increased . . . The hissing gathered speed, was travelling towards him, expanding, a deep sound within himself, between his ears, like the noises in a dream . . .

"Who are you?" he whispered, still holding the brittle skull to his forehead.

"I'll lead you out of here and to freedom if you promise to release me," the voice said in his head . . .

Diamond Books by Andrew Laurance

THE BLACK HOTEL
OUIJA
CATACOMB

BLOOD OF NOSTRADAMUS: THE PREMONITION
(coming in May)

CATACOMB

ANDREW LAURANCE

Originally published as *The Hiss*

DIAMOND BOOKS, NEW YORK

This book was originally published under
the title *The Hiss* in 1981 in Great Britain
by W.H. Allen & Co. Ltd.

CATACOMB

A Diamond Book/published by arrangement with
the author

PRINTING HISTORY
Star edition published 1981
Diamond edition/February 1991

All rights reserved.
Copyright © 1981 by Andrew Laurance. This book may not be reproduced in whole or in part, by mimeograph or any other means, without permission. For information address: The Berkley Publishing Group, 200 Madison Avenue, New York, New York 10016.

ISBN: 1-55773-460-7

Diamond Books are published by The Berkley Publishing Group,
200 Madison Avenue, New York, New York 10016.
The name "DIAMOND" and its logo are trademarks
belonging to Charter Communications, Inc.

PRINTED IN THE UNITED STATES OF AMERICA

10 9 8 7 6 5 4 3 2 1

CHAPTER
— 1 —

For the third morning running Juan awoke before the matins bell.

From the amount of light that came through the tiny window of his cell, he guessed it was about half past four, a half hour of guaranteed peace before Brother Martin burst in and switched on the light to make sure he was awake.

The monk would then stand there mumbling his rosary, watching him while he doused his eyes with water, sponged down his body and slipped on his tunic before kneeling in front of the crucifix to thank his Maker for having seen him safely through the night.

He made a face at that thought. He was beginning to have doubts about his Maker. He was beginning to have doubts and he was beginning to question everything he had been taught. Only a few days before he had calculated that soon it would be his seventeenth birthday and he had wondered what other boys of his age had experienced in the great outside world that he had not, and how much more he would have learned if he had not been sent to the brothers of the Dominitian Monastery at Monte Trasimeno.

He rubbed his young limbs under the coarse blanket and decided that he would not indulge himself again for at least forty eight hours, such self-imposed exhaustion was best left to the private moments before going to sleep. Besides, he was a little frightened of having another bad dream.

They were not always bad, but sometimes his dreams had been fearful and real enough for him to confess his self-abuse, which always pleased Brother Ignatius who would of course absolve him with lowered eyes and two fingers raised in the sign of the cross.

A lecture would follow, inevitably, but he would be forgiven for he was but a novice.

Now he heard the train in the far distance and got up to stand on the end of his pallet to see out of the tiny window. Below was a sheer drop of some sixty feet. Two miles away in the valley, he saw the dawn-pink buildings of Trasimeno and the winding necklace of lights of the Rome express.

Inside, people would be sitting and dozing the journey away, or lying on those lovely bunks under the disposable paper sheets, wrapped like corpses, never to understand the joys of their freedom unless they were suddenly incarcerated within a monastery like himself. He was a prisoner. Had been for three years. Three wasted years?

In fairness, no. Father Anthony had seen to that, had discussed it openly. Without Father Anthony he would have been bored and restless and might have even run away, but the Order had acknowledged his intelligence and his potential and put him in the hands of the gentle tutor who taught him Latin, Greek, some Mathematics and Classical History. He would be able to go to University if he chose to leave.

But then they had not taught him one word of Italian. "It will help you keep your vows of silence," he had been told. But he felt sure there was more to it than that.

How many foreigners like himself were there in the Order? None.

He was the only one to be given lessons, the subjects naturally helping to indoctrinate him in the Faith, and until he took the first vows of priesthood he would neither be allowed to speak or be spoken to directly by anyone but his Tutor, the Abbot, Brother Ignatius his confessor, and His Emminence the Visiting Cardinal Gregory.

He got down from the window, having watched the train disappear into the distance, and lay down on his pallet again. Would he enjoy lying on a normal mattress? Father Anthony had said not. Father Anthony had said that when he had had the occasion to lie on a spring mattress his bones and muscles had ached all the following day.

It would be nice to have a soft pillow however, as he had had at home. And he deliberately stopped himself thinking further. The memory of home, his childhood, was painful, and the vision of his grandfather was still with him, and of his grandmother and his Nanny Magdalena.

The ghosts. The phantoms of death. The decaying, melting skin across the bone structures of the face. The hollow holes instead of eyes, the grey-green gangrened flesh on the hands.

Their deaths had followed so shortly after the apparitions. He took a deep breath and turned over, pushed his head under the straw bolster. That was really why he was here.

"Within the sacred walls of a holy monastery evil spirits will no longer haunt you, they will not dare." That was what his aunt had told him, and it had been a lie.

He had only been eight years old when it had first happened. It was early morning, he was alone in the garden behind the large house outside Buenos Aires. He remembered little of it except its whiteness, and the stables with all the horses and Paco who looked after them, and his Nanny Magdalena.

The dew was on the green lawn, the lawn so well cared

for, his grandfather's pride. The water sprinklers switched on every morning before the sun got round the house where, in the heat of summer, he would go out and dance about in the silver spray.

That morning he had gone out alone wearing his yellow swimsuit, Magdalena busy upstairs tidying the nursery, his grandfather lying in bed sick, having fallen ill the week before.

Then the old man had appeared unexpectedly on the balcony overlooking the lawn, waving his stick. He had been wrapped in a white towelling dressing gown and had leaned heavily on the balustrade to watch him dance in the water. Juan had put on a special performance, instinctively feeling it would amuse the old man to see his youthful cavorting.

And jumping about as close to the sprinkler as was possible, the spray splashing his dark skin, Juan had looked up to smile at his grandfather and had seen the hideousness of death, a decaying face sticky with yellowish slime, one eye mucous white, the other a deep hole, but staring at him, and a set of clenched grey teeth smiling from a brown skull. Skeletal fingers gripped the curve of the cane and the other hand of parchment skin, stretched sinews and bones beckoned.

He had screamed. He had bellowed out his fear.

Magdalena and Paco had appeared from nowhere, rushed to him as he stood paralysed with terror.

The apparition had straightened up, turned and disappeared into the house silently. Paco had picked Juan up and carried him away from the spraying water.

No one could guess what had frightened him.

Paco had switched the sprinkler off and examined it. Magdalena had dried him, his grandmother had come out to see what had happened, the whole household on the balcony looking down.

CATACOMB

He had pointed to his grandfather's room, had uttered to or three words "Ghost... death... skull..." something like that, and everyone had hushed him up, had blanched, the maids crossing themselves.

Two days later the old man had died peacefully in his sleep.

He turned over and stared at the ceiling, then over again to hide under the blanket. Brother Martin would come in soon and switch on the light and stare at him, then the image would go away. One night he would sleep without his white cotton underpants and really give the dirty old monk an evil shock.

"Brother Joseph do you not think that our new young Brother Juan has a pretty face, like a girl's?"

"Shame on you Brother Martin, such thoughts are sinful."

"I have already confessed them to the Abbot."

He was not sure that that was exactly what had been said in front of him one morning during his first week at the monastery, but the following day they had cut his long jet black hair very short and he had not seen himself since then, except of course in the reflection of the water in the lavatory bowl. Mirrors were not allowed.

He was wide awake now, yet everything was so quiet he could have been in a dream. He did not like this airless sensation, it reminded him too much of the moments that preceded his walking into the bedroom where his grandmother had been laid out a few hours after her death.

What *had* happened? What *had* triggered off the horror he could not remember?

The green mucous slime mingled with blood on his hands and the sickly smell which stuck to his fingers for days afterwards, this he remembered. The twitching body, convulsing itself into life from the wet bed and suddenly jack-knifing, this he remembered. His own uncontrollable howling when he went mad with fear as the spattered walls were feverishly cleaned to remove any evidence of the manic occurance, this he remembered.

But what had happened before, what had happened after? That was all forgotten.

Had they drugged him heavily with sedatives, had he eventually gone to sleep? He had no recall, but he remembered the warning, the inexplicable lull before the storm which is what he was feeling now, the sensation that something inevitable was going to happen, something he would dread because of the stillness around him, because he was feeling so very peaceful, so very calm.

He heard the shuffle of Brother Martin's feet just outside the door and froze, closed his eyes, feigned sleep.

The door opened, the light went on. In a few seconds there would be the tap on the shoulder, and he would turn round and go through the motions of awakening, perhaps stretching one leg out, looking up at Brother Martin and smiling.

But Brother Martin took a long time before waking him. He could feel him close by looking down, staring at the folds of the blanket moulding his slim form. Brother Martin had been an artist, or so Father Anthony had said, and the study of human anatomy, as an artist, was not totally forbidden. After all, had not Michelangelo and Leonardo and Fra Angelico depicted saints and the Holy family by studying form?

The tap came on the right shoulder. He stirred, put his hand up to his mouth to hide a pretended yawn, turned over on his back and stretched.

He smiled, opened his eyes and gasped. Brother Martin had no lips, no teeth, his nose was but a cavity and his eyes were just a film of glutinous white mucous lining the sockets of a bony-grey death mask.

Juan cowered back as the fearful apparition stared at him. Slowly, very slowly, an expression formed on the hideous face, a questioning expression came into the eyes which now took shape within the mask, a twisted smile danced on the lips that appeared where there had been none.

Juan got up, side stepped the monk to pour cold water from the jug into the basin and splashed his face.

Temporarily blinded he reached for the towel, dried himself and looked over his shoulder at Brother Martin.

The man was no ghost, he was all there now, whole, alive, nothing to be afraid of.

Another apparition then? After all this time they were starting again, within the precincts of Holy seclusion? The warnings of imminent death?

Juan slipped on his white tunic, tied the cord tight round his middle, slipped his feet into the canvas sandals then knelt down in front of the wooden crucifix on the wall behind the door.

"If there is a God who can hear me," he said in his head, "then please explain these manifestations, tell me why I have to be frightened like this. If I take the final vows will I be spared such experiences? Is it really a sign, the evil within me trying to get out as the Abbot Father has suggested?"

He made the sign of the cross and stood up.

The morning routine followed. Matins in the twelfth-century chapel with its frescoes behind the altar attributed to Masaccio, its existence known only to those who entered the walls of the monastery.

The first meal of the day. The breakfast of milk, bread

and honey. The Order was strictly vegetarian, not even eggs nor fish were ever eaten.

The monastery was self-sufficient, with its own cows for milk and cheese, its own fields of corn and maize, its own orchards and vegetable gardens. The regime was simple: prayers, reading, manual work and eating in common, sleeping in cells six hours in the twenty-four.

Across the refectory at the end of the high table sat Father Anthony, pious, thoughtful. A teacher priest from an abbey school in Glastonbury, he had joined the Dominitians but a few months before Juan had arrived, for reasons he had never revealed.

In the centre of the table, like Jesus Christ at the Last Supper, was the Abbot, his white pointed beard suggesting a deal of vanity, an actor, lording it over his troupe of sinners. Then fat Brother Ignatius the monastery treasurer, ever scheming, disliked by most, Juan sensed, despite the vows of silence, holier and more pious than the Pope himself, when necessary.

Today, Saturday, like every other day, Juan would clean and dust the Abbot's study, then Brother Ignatius's after which he would join Father Anthony in the library schoolroom for his lessons.

As he stood at the long refectory table, he reflected that he had no one on earth to turn to if he should leave this establishment. Both his grandparents had wanted him to become a priest, his grandmother's dearest wish had been that he should be appointed to the Vatican. They were dead. Because of this wish of hers he had always been obedient and good, had told people that he was committed to the church though it was not true.

His aunt, his mother's sister, had not dissuaded him when he had become their responsibility, rather the contrary. There had been visits to the doctors of course, and to the child psychoanalyst who had become his friend and had perceived that he was not that sincere in his religious beliefs, but the church had eventually taken him over. He was sent to St Anselm's, the Roman Catholic College, where, for the first time, he had been made aware by other boys that he was an orphan. Both his parents had been killed in a plane crash when he was but a baby. His friends had liked him for that, they thought it dramatic. But it had only made him feel different.

In this community he was younger than everyone else, by at least ten years. He had to remember how safe he had felt when he had first arrived, how grateful. Now, because he was older and getting restless, could he discard that feeling? Apparently not. The vision of Brother Martin was a reminder of what awaited him outside, that was all. It was a reminder of what he would see around every corner if he left the sacred safety of these hallowed walls.

And what would he do in the great big world anyway? If he ever got out? Maybe, as he had so often been told, he *had* been chosen by the Lord to serve him. But he just did not believe that.

That there was a power, an infinite power, a massive unimaginable brain somewhere in the ether which controlled everything, he might believe that. That there had been a very great man called Jesus Christ who had come on earth for a while like Mohammed and Buddha and taught the people of their time, he believed that, but that they were supernatural, he could not believe that. He could not agree with the monks, who pretended humility but deep down believed themselves superior to most men, that God, the Son of God and the Mother of God actually listened to their prayers because they were of the Order of Saint Dominitian. And Father Anthony was of the same opinion, though of course he could not say so.

Juan stood and waited with all the others for the Abbot to say Grace, then they all sat down on the creaking benches and broke the bread, literally, and sipped their cold milk.

They were all supposed to listen to the monk who stood at the lectern reading, but most did not. They munched and drank and thought about their petty problems.

If he wanted to he could probably escape in the night, though the two main doors were usually locked and the surrounding walls pretty high. He could request to leave, but there would be legal problems. His Aunt and Uncle had virtually committed him to the monastery till he was eighteen.

Perhaps he would become a Cardinal and eventually the Pope. But then for that he would have to satisfy the authorities that he believed in the Immaculate Conception, which cast so much doubt in his mind, and the resurrection from the dead! Could people return? Could they come back in their own shape or someone else's, be reborn, reincarnated?

Breakfast was over, all the brothers stood up after grace, everyone scurried off to their cells to clean up and make their beds. It was the last moment in his day when he could be alone, until bed-time when, exhausted, he usually fell on his pallet and went straight to sleep.

What was it that deep inside him made him feel so different to his fellow beings, even different to Father Anthony. The ghosts? The premonitions of other people's deaths?

The bell sounded for lauds.

In the chapel he stood, knelt, he stood again and knelt again.

Though he had been too young to remember either of his parents because of the accident, his mother had been made to exist for him, had been talked about, whereas his father had not. There was quite a lot of death around him, when he came to think of it.

And as he stood again, listening to the chanting of the

Abbot's voice, he tried to imagine the accident again. His father, his mother, returning to Buenos Aires from New York: the silver airliner taking off, losing height, suddenly plummeting into the sea, never to be found. He was in the Buenos Aires house, four months old, cradled and fed by Magdalena, his paternal grandparents already dead in their native Columbia far away. Peru, he had been told once, then it had changed to Columbia, later he had heard that he was of pure Spanish stock from Sevilla. It had all added up to a great mystery.

He had decided, finally, that maybe his mother had not married at all, but had had an affair with a man who was not regarded by the Montoneros family as good enough for their delicate daughter, and they had tried to hush it all up.

That she had died in a plane crash, he accepted, that his father was with her was probable, anyway all he had to do was go to a records office somewhere in New York and check, which was one of his ambitions.

His secret ambitions.

He walked along the novices' cloister and up the wide stairs to the scriptorium, the library where the very smell of books was an enchantment. The wooden shelves creaked under the weight of the volumes there ready to be read. At least he had been taught the value of reading and had that longing to become the wisest man on earth. He came to the schoolroom door and knocked.

"Come in!"

Father Anthony was sitting by the window. The morning sun blazed in over the back of his tutor's head spotlighting the slightly stained blackness of his cassock.

Father Anthony was reading Caxton's Chronicles of England again, so homesick he was. He looked up briefly, acknowledgement in his eyes that he was pleased to see him.

"Sit down Juanito," he said warmly.

Juan sat down at the table in the middle of the room and opened up the large wooden box in which he kept his exercise books, his pencils, his ball-point pen, treasures which he was not allowed to have in his own cell for no personal possessions were permitted.

"Did you sleep well?" Father Anthony asked, closing his book loudly and standing up to stretch in front of the window.

"Yes thank you Father." They were the first words he had uttered that morning.

"And did you dream?"

"No."

"I had a dream," Father Anthony said, "I dreamt that the Abbot cut half his beard off while shaving and asked me to stick the shorn hairs back on again with glue."

It was a mischievous jab, which both enjoyed, Juan not sure whether the dream was true. It was as far as mischief against authority would ever be allowed to go, but it was a relief.

"You're looking very troubled," Father Anthony said sitting down in the armchair opposite, leaning right across the table. "Have you any problems?"

"I did have a dream," he admitted.

"Tell! Tell, Juanito, dear heart. Dreams are our only escape and an insight into our yearnings." Father Anthony put his elbows together on the top of the table and rested his chin on his clasped hands and waited.

"I dreamt . . . that I saw Brother Martin as a ghost, as a dead man, as a living yet dead figure."

Father Anthony's expression changed. A seriousness came into his eyes though he stayed in the same position so as not to show emotion. "What did he do?"

"Nothing. He just stood there in my room when he woke me up."

"When he woke you up in your dream?"

Juan hesitated. "It wasn't quite a dream," he admitted.

Father Anthony straightened up, leaned back in his armchair, put his hand to his mouth to bite a nail. "You saw an *apparition* of Brother Martin?"

"I don't think it was an apparition. An apparition suggests that it was unreal, insubstantial . . . Brother Martin was there, only instead of being himself, he was his own corpse."

"Like your grandfather?"

The question was astonishing. He had never told anyone about the vision of his grandfather, anyone but the family and the doctor who had examined him.

"You didn't know I knew?" Father Anthony asked, surprised.

The priest had made a mistake and was aware of it, he had given away the fact that all this time he had had knowledge of his unstable background, of the fearful nightmares he had had of the haunting sight of the ghost walking the balcony and of his grandfather dying.

"Of course I did not know," Juan said. He did not mean to sound so hurt, but the surprise he felt at the deception was in his voice.

Father Anthony got up, brusquely, and walked over to the window. It was as though the temperature in the room had dropped, as if a veil had come between them, or was about to come down between them and that they would have to fight to push it out of the way.

Father Anthony was fighting it, fighting something. His fingers behind his back were interlaced, moving nervously.

"It was a deliberate mistake, Juan, my mentioning the vision you had of your grandfather. It was a carefully rehearsed mistake which I have been waiting to use for quite some time." He turned to face Juan. "You will have been with us three years next Tuesday, and I have to submit a report to the Vatican authorities about the state of your mental health. I am not only your tutor, you see, I am also your examiner."

"You still think me mad?"

"I do not. I neither think you mad nor simple, nor over imaginative. I think you are an intelligent young man who has seen something that few others have ever seen, and know that I will be unable to convince my superiors that this is important, because it hardly fits in with their doctrine," Father Anthony turned to look out of the window.

"I saw Brother Martin this morning as a walking dead," Juan repeated, wanting to be believed. "The same as I saw my grandfather and Brother Bonamente."

Father Anthony whipped round. "You saw Brother Bonamente as a living corpse?"

"Two days before he died."

"Did you tell anyone of this?"

"I have taken the vow of silence with everyone but yourself and your superiors."

"Would you interpret this morning's vision as a premonition of death, then?"

"Yes."

"But Brother Martin is a healthy young man."

"I am not inventing it, it is what I saw."

Father Anthony closed his eyes, clasped his hands before him and raised his head slightly upwards in way of prayer. "I need guidance, I so badly need guidance on this." Father Anthony opened his eyes and turned to look at Juan.

"How many days, usually, between the vision and the death?"

"With my grandfather it was two or three days, with my grandmother three, with Magdalena a few hours, with

Brother Bonamente at least a week. I don't think there is a rule or a pattern."

"Why did you not mention your vision of Brother Bonamente to me before?"

"I had no reason to do so. Besides, I wanted to forget, I came here to forget, and he died very shortly after I arrived here."

"Is this apparition of Brother Martin the first you have had in three years then?"

"Yes."

"Brother Xavier died last year. What of him?"

"I did not know him."

"The visions are only of people you know?"

"I meant I never met Brother Xavier. The visions are usually metamorphoses of people standing close to me."

Father Anthony started to pace the room. "Brother Bonamente was an old man, very old . . . Where did you see him?"

"In the cloister leading to the refectory."

"Anyone else?" Father Anthony asked.

"No," Juan said.

"I should report this you understand, but I will not." Father Anthony said. "I will wait, if you can promise me this." He sat down opposite Juan and leaned across the table.

"Should Brother Martin die . . ." He quickly crossed himself, "Should he die, you must not contradict me when I report to the authorities that you only told me of the vision *after* he was dead."

"I have taken the vow of silence."

"Your vow of silence will be lifted next Tuesday in all probability, besides you may be questioned by His Emminence."

And it was the way it was said, the fear, it seemed, in Father Anthony's voice which was unsettling. It was clear now that all along his tutor had been a great deal more than just a tutor, he had been an investigator.

"We should proceed with your lessons now," Father Anthony said, standing up again, the master in control, the disciplinarian.

Juan opened up his box and took out *The Education of a Christian Prince* and opened it on the marked page.

As he was about to remind Father Anthony where they had got to, the Angelus sounded, a slow steady clanging of the death knoll.

Father Anthony looked up, staring at him.

There was a knock at the door, and then it opened. The Abbot stood there, sadness masking his face. "Brother Martin," he said in a low whisper.

"Of what?" Father Anthony asked.

"A heart attack it seems. He was in the kitchen. He was cleaning the vegetables and collapsed."

The Abbot closed his eyes, then opened them again to look at Juan. "Heaven gives its favourites early death," he said. "Sometimes without warning."

CHAPTER
— 2 —

The service was short, a few words spoken by the Abbot, and it was simply a question of kneeling and listening. Tomorrow there would be the burial service, and on Sunday a requiem mass.

Juan thought of the vision of Brother Martin seen not eight hours ago, thought of his grandfather, grandmother, Magdalena and Brother Bonamente.

Premonitions, Father Anthony had suggested. He wasn't sure about that, premonitions were surely warnings that could be acted on. These visions were not that.

Was he here instead of an institution, had he been sent all the way to Italy so that the family could be rid of the embarrassment of a lunatic? Or were they attempting to cure him through religion? He closed his eyes to observe the demanded silence.

The vision of Magdalena's death was still as vivid as though it had happened yesterday.

He had woken up in his room in New York where they had all moved for the winter. The apartment overlooked Central Park, and his room, facing an older building across the street, had the sun coming in brightly that morning because it had been snowing and all was white.

Normally Magdalena came into the room and woke him up, but that morning she had not. He had stirred, rather late, and had got dressed, sensing that something must be wrong. He had gone through the green baize door to the servants' quarters and to the room where Magdalena slept. Magdalena was lying in bed looking very pale.

"Don't come in niño. I am not well and until the doctor has come to see me it is not wise. What if I have something contagious?"

He had left feeling sorry for her, yet relieved that he would be alone all day.

He had been driven across New York to St Anselm's College by Carlos and this new routine over the week had made everyone realize that Magdalena was no longer necessary, that he should be looked after by a man and no longer a nanny.

Three weeks or so later he learned that Magdalena was to be moved to hospital and had gone to her room to wish her well. On entering he had recoiled from the fearful sight of her lying on the bed. Her face, unlike his grandfather's, had not been a skull but a decayed head, wet, sticky, the jaw muscles taut, bluish, the veins over the forehead pulsating, the eyes bulbous, the hair long, white, unkempt.

The shock had rooted him as the eyes stared at him all-knowing. He had not screamed that time, he had just stared at the fearful vision, the decaying corpse sitting up in bed.

But then he had fainted, had found himself on the couch in the drawing room being sponged down by Carlos, his tightlipped aunt standing close by, pale, frightened.

"What happened Juan?" Carlos had asked. "What happened?"

"Magdalena is going to die," he had said, simply.

Carlos had closed his eyes and crossed himself and his

aunt had said, quite tersely "He's mad . . ." and had left the room.

That night Magdalena had died, and her death had quite obviously sealed his fate. Her funeral was attended only by the servants and himself, a black and white snow scene by the graveside. When he returned to the warm apartment, Father Brian from St Anselm's had been waiting for him in the drawing room to question him on what he had seen.

The service ended and Juan waited his turn to leave the row of pews, looking forward to going back to the schoolroom to talk over what had happened, but Brother Ignatius was waiting for him by the doors and tapped him on the shoulder, a particularly irritating way of communication, the very tip of his sharp nail digging into the back.

With his other hand he was holding tightly onto Brother Patrice and made it clear that instead of going back to his studies he was to accompany the morose monk to the infirmary.

Brother Patrice was the monk whom everyone avoided, partly because of his smell, because he was death's representative in the monastery. It was he who prepared the bodies for burial, made the coffins and dug the graves, and though Juan at first thought that he had been designated to help Brother Patrice in way of punishment—for goodness knows what—he realized as he made his way to the infirmary, that it was probably so that his reaction to the dead man could be watched.

Father Anthony had obviously spoken to the Abbot and they had decided in their infinite wisdom that helping wash down the corpse might well cure him of his hallucinations.

In his own kingdom, Brother Patrice won Juan's respect. In the small whitewashed mortuary room with its stone sinks, polished brass taps and shelves of disinfectants, he moved quickly and efficiently, knowing exactly what he was doing.

Brother Martin's body clothed in a white tunic was laid on a marble slab in the centre of the room.

Juan was first asked to hold him up so that the sleeves could be drawn off and the tunic removed. The body was surprisingly heavy.

The mouth hung open, the eyes were firmly closed and Brother Patrice worked incredibly quickly. For such work the vow of silence was lifted so that Brother Patrice could give him instructions.

"Lift him up by the shoulders while I remove his underpants, then we'll turn him over and wrap him up in the shroud." So Brother Patrice was English, or did he detect a definite Irish accent?

"Roll him over on his left side now, Brother Juan."

The tunic was off, he was holding the naked body of a middle aged man with white skin, flabby round the stomach and rather hairy.

Brother Patrice held a bottle of surgical spirit and with cotton wool cleaned the whole body, the forehead, the nose, the neck, inside the ears, the shoulders, under the armpits, along the arms, along each finger of each hand, the chest, round in the crotch lifting the penis as though it was no different to anything else, not looking up, in no way embarrassed. The legs, the knees, under the feet, between each toe.

"Turn him on the stomach now, the poor soul."

The same, the back of the neck, behind the ears, down the spine, pouring the spirit in the hollows, sponging him down, the buttocks, between the buttocks where it was hairy, the back of the legs, the ankles, the heels. He then started to clean the nails.

"They grow you know. The nails and hair go on growing

for a while. Not everything dies when the soul leaves the body. Now we can roll him up in the shroud."

As Brother Patrice unfolded a length of clean white linen and stretched it along half of the marble slab to roll the body onto it, the door opened and two other brothers came in with trestles, and two more came in carrying a pinewood coffin.

The coffin was lined with white material, nothing fancy, but it looked comfortable enough. They all helped to lift the body and place it in the box, everyone crossing themselves after the effort.

Brother Patrice arranged the head, tucking the shroud in around the feet and under the legs, then he seemed satisfied enough that a good job had been done.

The lid was placed on the coffin, but the screws were not turned, and the two monks took it out as Juan stood back while Brother Patrice washed down the slab of marble with water and surgical spirit and afterwards mopped the stone floor.

Why had he been asked to help? Had they expected him to have seen Brother Martin as a ghost again, react, scream, as he had with his grandfather? Faint as he had with Magdalena?

He would probably never be told, but he would ask. From now on he would ask, and from Father Anthony's answers, or rather his refusals to answer, he would gather something.

There was nothing unusual about Father Anthony's attitude towards him during the afternoon lessons, Latin translations and text comparisons.

"Interea medium aeneas iam classe tenebat . . . Meanwhile now with purpose fixed Aeneas . . ."

"Meanwhile Aeneas, his purpose fixed," Father Anthony corrected.

"Meanwhile Aeneas . . ." Juan stopped, looked at his tutor.

"Well go on."

"Why was I sent to help Brother Patrice?"

"You know I can't answer that."

"But you can tell me if the reason was connected with me seeing Brother Martin as a vision this morning."

"I can tell you that, yes. But I am not sure that I should."

"Which is an answer in itself."

"That is for you to interpret. Back to Mr Virgil, please."

"Why do you think I saw the vision?"

"I don't know," Father Anthony said, "I really don't know. But I want you to do something for me and for yourself. I want you to go about your day as though absolutely nothing extraordinary had happened. The other brothers are going to look at you more than they have, a whisper, a gossip is bound to have got around about what happened, they always do."

"Because Brother Ignatius chatters?" Juan suggested.

"Because there is little else to think about in such a small community . . ." It was the first time Father Anthony had allowed himself to voice a criticism, however slight.

"I have a plan," he went on, "I want to try something out with you which requires leaving the monastery. To get permission you *must* behave loyally. Brother Ignatius is determined to label you a rebel, don't give him cause."

Brother Martin's coffin was placed before the chapel altar for the next twenty-four hours.

As was the custom, two monks were to stay all night and all day with the body and as Juan expected, he was ordered to act out the night vigil.

Did they now expect him to see Brother Martin rise out of the coffin?

The night was long, cold and very tedious. Four candles burned at each corner of the open box, a wooden crucifix resting on the dead man's stomach.

The other monk was relieved at four in the morning, but he was not, an obvious sign that he was being singled out.

He was allowed to go to his cell after matins and breakfast and he lay down on the pallet and fell asleep.

It was Brother Patrice who woke him up three hours later with a glass of water and made a sign conveying that the burial service was soon to begin.

He seemed to be living in the chapel. Prayers were mumbled and the monks passed the coffin in single file to pay the last personal tribute to a fellow brother.

Juan looked into the coffin. The monk's face was now alabaster white, the eyes were closed, the lips pursed, the expression that of intense pain in death. He seemed altogether smaller, shrunken and his hair was grey, brittle. The skin on his long proud hands was shrivelled and the colour of yellowed parchment.

Juan felt a revulsion at the thought of brushing a dutiful kiss on the stone cold lips, afraid that he might recoil with disgust, but he was drawn to it, compelled to do it.

He leaned down, holding his breath, and pressed his forehead against the dead man's brow.

The hiss was like air escaping from a cavity deep within the skull. It was a whisper penetrating the labyrinth of his own mind, a message of unintelligible, separate words that slowly gained clarity.

"Help me Brother Juan . . ." the voice of the dead rasped. *"Help . . . me and all of us . . ."*

His was the power to communicate with the dead?

"We will call on you Juan . . . I will call on you . . . if you do not come . . ."

And theirs the power to make him do so?

He pulled away, glanced around to look if anyone had seen a reaction. It seemed not. He walked on, back to his pew, back to his prayers till it was time to get up again and follow the coffin out to the little cemetery with its graves marked only by simple wrought iron crosses and the hole, the deep, deep, hole.

The Abbot, in black, sang-out the last rites, enjoying the drama of the occasion. Ashes to ashes, dust to dust, the earth was piled on and it was over.

As they filtered back through into the monastery, Father Anthony, Brother Ignatius and the Abbot were waiting for him. The Abbot laid a hand on his shoulder to stop his progress.

"Tomorrow, Brother Ignatius," he said in his strong Italian accent, addressing the monastery's treasurer, "Tomorrow, Father Anthony and Brother Juan will be going with me to visit the Hospital of Santa Cecilia in Rome. You will arrange for transport."

"Of course."

"We will leave after matins, after *prima colazione.*"

The heavy hand was lifted from his shoulder and he was allowed to proceed back to his cell where half an hour of solitary meditation had been prescribed to speed Brother Martin heavenward.

There were so many things Juan had not seen for so long and so many new things, new signs on the road, new vehicles, new motorbikes, the advertisements, the people, that the two hour drive to Rome seemed to last a quarter of that time.

He sat between the two fathers in the back of a black limousine with white lace curtains across the rear window as they sped through the Umbrian countryside. Women crossed themselves on seeing a car of the Holy See. It made him feel important.

They were entering Rome now, passing the pink and yellow tenement buildings with faded green shutters and washing hanging from every conceivable place. Juan was entranced by the dust, the traffic, the noise, the excitement of city life. He wanted to get out and be among it all, it would be terrible going back to the monastery after this.

The Santa Cecilia Hospital, run by nuns of the Holy Order of Santa Cecilia, was within a short walk from the South wall of the Vatican's Congregation of the Doctrine of the Faith.

They climbed the steps of the old building and went into the silent marbled hallway with its domed ceiling and majestical stairway and its nuns gliding up and down it as though it were a giant escalator. A Mother Superior greeted them and led them swiftly to the top of the stairway, through modern swing doors with polished brass fittings, down a passage which smelt of ether and into a ward.

There were twenty beds, some curtained off. Lying in each of them was an elderly man wearing a blue nightshirt, each sickly pale and more yellowish of skin than the next.

They walked very slowly down the aisle, pausing at each bed as the Mother Superior explained the illness. Juan still had no idea why he was there. Then the doors behind them opened and a nun came in leading a young girl, about his own age, quite beautiful. She was pale, with the blackest of hair done up in tresses and somehow tied behind her head in a bun. She reminded him of one of Botticelli's angels. She wore a simple grey dress with a white lace collar, a black belt and flat black shoes. She was sad, nervous and as she was taken to the bed of one of the old men she smiled bravely at Father Anthony as though she knew him.

Juan stood behind the Abbot and Father Anthony as the

Mother Superior explained something else in whispers as they stood at the bed of the thinnest man Juan had ever seen. But it was not this patient who caught his eye, it was the larger, fatter man in the neighbouring bed. He tried to avoid looking at him, but could not.

The man was sitting up, propped up by pillows, his hands crossed over an ample stomach and Juan first noticed the hands because they were stubby bones, with tell-tale skeletal joints.

Then as he stared at the face there was a gradual change. The skin changed first, from a surprisingly healthy pink to an ashen grey, then the tissues wrinkled, shrivelled, the skin across the forehead tightened till it silently snapped, exposing polished bone. Then one eye, just one eye, seemed to fall back into the skull cavity, and a fearful worm crawled up and out along the edge of the orifice.

It was so disgusting, so repellent, that Juan uncontrollably turned on his heels to face the other way, catching his breath. Both the Abbot and Father Anthony turned to look at him, and the Mother Superior raised her eyebrows at such unseeming behaviour.

He felt sick, he felt the vomit coming up inside him, like that worm, tickling him at the back of the throat. If he was made to look at the man again he would faint as he had on seeing Magdalena.

He felt the Abbot's firm hand on his shoulder. "Are you unwell Brother Juan? What have you seen that causes you such distress?"

That was why he had been brought here then. He should have guessed. It was in the victorious look in Father Anthony's eyes. He had been brought here especially as a test. He had been brought here to see if he could predict a death, to check whether he had these occult, these magical powers!

"Have you seen anything unusual?" Father Anthony asked, a pained expression of sympathy in his eyes.

"Yes," he said in a whisper.

The Abbot put his arm round his shoulder and led him further down the aisle between the beds. It had all been planned, worked out. If the boy was psychic, as Father Anthony claimed, then his psychic powers should be tested. Take him to where the dying are and see what happens.

They were passing the bed where the beautiful girl was sitting, curtained off now during the visit. He must have hesitated, made a movement as though to look between the curtains because the Abbot suggested they should be allowed to see the patient.

Juan did not want to look at the man, he just wanted to see the girl again. They were the same age: youth surrounded by the aged and dying. There was an affinity between them.

The Mother Superior drew back the curtain and the girl immediately stood up. He looked at her, stared at her, wanting to remember her, take the memory of her back to his cell. He could love such a girl, adore her.

The Mother Superior said something gentle in Italian and the girl sat down, her hands loosely clasped in her lap, her feet together. She could be sixteen, seventeen, no older. He looked at the old man in the bed next to her. What he saw was total decay, a decomposition he could not have imagined. The man was a complete skeleton, a skull and rib cage lying loosely in the bed. No horror, this time, no tissues, no nerves or muscles or skin, just the bones, off-white, dry, complete death.

"He has grown very weak in the last twenty-four hours," the Mother Superior said in English so that the girl would not understand.

But she did understand. A very slight smile crossed her

delicate lips, an amused expression came into her eyes. She was thankful that the Mother had tried not to hurt her feelings, but she had understood. The Mother drew the curtain across. Would he never see her again?

Luncheon was served to them in a small room on the third floor. It was a marvellous meal of pasta with cheese and spinach, and ice cream to follow, all within the allowed vows.

They were waited on by two nuns, novices, and he was astonished to see how openly the Abbot flirted with them, stared at them as they moved, and how they in turn knowing this turned a smart ankle on leaving the room. Was there so much hypocrisy in this church?

"What then made you react so strongly in the ward, Juan?" Father Anthony asked when the nuns had left.

He described what he had seen, he described it very fully, staring at Father Anthony and timing the description so that the mention of the worm coincided with the Abbot lifting his pasta-piled fork up to his mouth.

The Abbot appreciated what he was trying to do, smiled and managed to put the forkful of long spaghetti in his mouth. "And does that signify something to you, do you presume that he will die, this fat man, shortly?" The Abbot asked.

"I don't know."

"Was this last vision the same as that of Brother Martin?"

"No."

"In what way was it different?"

"It was more frightening."

"Does that mean anything, do you think?"

"I don't know."

The Abbot finished his plate of pasta, and Juan looked at his own spaghetti and realized he could not eat it. It was not that it reminded him of the worm, there was no connection, it was that he had just lost his appetite. The impact the beautiful girl had made on him was the trouble.

"Was there anyone else in the ward that looked as though they were dead?" Father Anthony asked.

"No," Juan lied.

"Why were you so interested in the man behind the curtain then?" the Abbot asked.

"I was not. I was interested in the girl."

The Abbot closed his eyes as though he were in the presence of something truly evil. "I trust you will remember that when you come to confession Brother Juan."

It was this incredible bigotry and total two-facedness that he could not understand. What harm did it do wanting to look at a pretty girl? And wasn't honesty ever to be rewarded? He wasn't sure he would be able to tolerate the monastery now. It had been a mistake for them to bring him out here.

"May I ask you a question Father?" Juan said to the Abbot.

"Of course you may, but it will not necessarily be answered."

"Why did you bring me here? Was it to test my ability to see death?"

"Your ability to see death? Is that what you call it?"

"That is what it seems to be."

The Abbot turned to Father Anthony whose duty it was to teach, to explain, to answer tricky questions.

"Yes Juan, it was," Father Anthony said. "You seem to have developed this ability as you call it, and we wanted to know how far it goes. It seems that the patient you saw in a state of death, though at present alive, *may* die shortly. If this is so, then it will confirm that you have certain unnatural instincts. That you have, for some reason, developed a sixth sense . . . which though not necessarily unique, *is* rare and should be examined further."

"Is that why I was brought to the Monastery of Saint Dominitian?" he asked the Abbot directly, who again looked at Father Anthony.

"No," his tutor answered. "You came to us because of your complete understanding and devotion to the Faith."

He was lying, Juan knew it, but Father Anthony stared straight at him defying him to argue in front of the Abbot. He said nothing therefore, but now knew he was getting closer to the mystery that was surrounding him.

When Juan joined Father Anthony the following day in the schoolroom for his lessons, he found his tutor particularly troubled. Father Anthony was sitting in his customary position, chin resting on clasped hands, elbows on the table, his brow frowning, his gaze vacant.

"Good morning Father."

"Hello Juan . . ."

Juan busied himself opening up the box, taking out his papers, his books. It was Greek this morning, Homer.

"When you see these people as dead," Father Anthony asked suddenly, "Do they move or are they still?"

"Oh . . . they move."

"Do they in any way give you the impression that they are communicating with you?"

"No. Not really."

"They just stand there and stare?"

"They stare, but they don't have eyes."

Father Anthony went back into his own shell and Juan took out his ball-point pen and started doodling on the pad he used for notes.

"We have never spoken of this seriously Juan," Father

Anthony said after a while, "But what do you think these apparitions are?"

"Warnings of death," Juan said simply.

He was not going to mention the hiss, he was not going to tell anyone that the visions were somehow connected with the already dead.

"Why do you think *you* get these warnings?"

"Perhaps warning is the wrong word," Juan said. "Warning suggests that I might be able to do something about it, but I can't. I think that for some reason I just see a change in the metabolism of the person who has started the process of dying before others can. That's all."

"And what of the people themselves. Do they know?"

"I expect so. I expect that when you are about to die you know within yourself that the end is near."

"How many people have you actually seen in this state?"

Juan did not answer immediately, he weighed up the consequences of telling the truth. Whatever he said would be repeated to the Abbot, then the Cardinal. But he had to answer. "Including the two people yesterday, seven."

"*Two* yesterday? You saw someone else?"

"Yes," Juan admitted, "The girl's father."

"Why didn't you tell us?"

"Because I felt sorry for the girl and I did not want any fuss made. I felt she was sufficiently upset."

"So you believe that the fat man and the girl's father are likely to die in the next few days?"

"Yes."

Father Anthony reverted to his pensive position, looking down at the table now, at the books, the pencils, the note pad. Juan doodled on, enlarging on the symbol he had drawn, that was taking shape, shading in the lines within a circle, making it look three dimensional.

"You mentioned seven," Father Anthony said, breaking

the silence. "There was your grandfather, grandmother, your Nanny, Brother Martin, Brother Bonamente and the two men yesterday. What did you see of Brother Bonamente?"

"I saw him walking down a cloister."

"And why were you afraid to speak about this to anyone?"

"Because I thought people would think me mad. I think I may have been sent here because of these visions, because my aunt and uncle did not understand what was happening, because it was an easier way out for them than sending me to a lunatic asylum."

Father Anthony smiled. "Is that how you see us here? As lunatics and the monastery an asylum?"

Juan shrugged. "I don't see the other brothers as lunatics, I see them as warders."

There was a knock on the door. Father Anthony got up to open it. Juan could not see who was on the other side, and could not understand the whispers either, but when Father Anthony closed the door he looked even more weary. "Signor Sciasia died three hours ago."

"Signor Sciasia?"

"The fat man in the hospital." Father Anthony sat down again at the table and pressed his thumbs hard against his clenched teeth.

Juan went on doodling. The symbol was growing hairs, roots and branches, the circle little thorns. It was not unlike the star of David but with nine points, three of which formed a triangle. It had a cabalistic feel about it, but meant nothing. He looked up to see Father Anthony studying him, studying what he was doing.

"What is that you've drawn?"

"A doodle."

"Have you doodled it before?"

"Once or twice."

"Where does it come from?"

"My head, I suppose."

"It's nothing special?"

"No . . ." He was rather amused by Father Anthony's concern.

"Have you seen it anywhere else, on a wall perhaps, in a book?"

"I may have done, but I don't remember."

"Would the word Octave mean anything to you?"

"Eight?" Juan said. "Of the musical scale?" he did not see the connection.

"Other than that?"

"No."

"A nine pointed star is odd."

Juan shrugged. Was it that Father Anthony was going a little off balance, had he been right in supposing the place was a funny farm?

He finished the doodle, adding scaffolding round the star, lengthening the scaffolding and placing it firmly on the side of a hill with dramatic shadows, adding two small figures looking up at it, so small that the whole construction was like a giant religious symbol.

He then tore the paper off the pad, screwed it up and dropped it in the wastebasket beside him. Looking up he saw Father Anthony staring at him even more intently. It was a look he had not seen before. It was the expression of someone staring at something in . . . awe. Studying an object he had had in his possession for quite some time without realizing its full value. The look gave him the feeling that he, Juan Ramirez Montoneros, was more than just a boy turned novice-monk, he was something unique.

"Do you know a lot about me Father, a lot more than I know about myself?"

"Possibly," the priest said.

"When I paid my last respects to Brother Martin in the chapel," Juan said, "He spoke to me."

Father Anthony raised an eyebrow slightly. "What did he say to you?"

"He said that I had to help him, help them, all of them, the dead."

The priest went on staring at him, curious.

"Do the dead know a lot about me?" Juan asked.

"Why don't you ask them?" Father Anthony answered.

CHAPTER
— 3 —

It was a dream.

Within it he knew it was not reality, but the ghosts were there, beckoning. His grandparents, Magdalena, Brother Bonamente and Brother Martin. They were all there threatening to haunt him if he did not act.

This was an inner knowledge. If he did not help them, did not do as they wished they would terrify him by their unexpected presence at every possible opportunity till he was rendered nervously insane. When he came out of the dream and thought he had woken up he felt that perhaps he had never been asleep, then a Latin phrase came to him, hummed in his mind.

Dilatio damnum habet, mora periculum. Procrastination brings loss, delay danger. It was from Erasmus, he had discussed its validity with Father Anthony. Now it was a message. *Act!*

And the idea of doing so, though it would be fearful, somehow intrigued him. There was a full moon, it would be possible. He lay on his pallet planning how he would go about it, then he got up on the end of the bed and stared out of the window. The dark landscape was ghostly with undefined shapes and shadows. To the North West there was the town with its dim street lights, evidence of life. Behind the monastery to the East was the monks' cemetery, evidence of death.

What if he was discovered? They could lock him up. It would give them the excuse to do so, but then was he not locked up already? No one in the whole wide world knew what had happened to him. His aunt and uncle had ceased to write to him years ago, he did not write to them. If they imprisoned him in a cell no one would care.

He got up, went to the door to listen. Not a sound. He took his brown novice's tunic down off the hook eased the door catch and pulled it open very slowly.

No noise, no creaks, no squeaks. He closed the door of his cell, and stole down the cloister on bare feet, holding his sandals.

He reached the garden door, slipped on his sandals and stepped out into the air. He was startled by the amount of light coming from the perfectly circular moon. It gave out no brightness but clarity with sharp shadows. The garden smelt delightfully of dama-de-noche, and it was all so fresh, the grass underfoot wet with dew, a sudden flutter of wings as he disturbed an owl.

The wrought iron gate in the garden wall was locked. He would have to climb the wall. The Abbot defended his privacy so much. Or perhaps it was to stop Brother Ignatius from going into the vegetable garden to steal raw onions. The fat old fool.

The trunk of an unexpected tree made him jump. It loomed up in front of him so suddenly that he thought it was a person. He reached for the lower branches and pulled himself up.

He hadn't climbed a tree since leaving Buenos Aires. Those were the days before he had started seeing the ghosts.

He was up in the tree now, and above the wall and could

see the military precision of the rows of vegetables in the fields beyond. The smells of the night were marvellous, magnificent, and he was two hundred metres from his goal. He found the top of the wall, now it was only a drop down.

He fell in some very soft earth where his footprints would give him away. It was darker down here now and he had to strain his eyes to see the lie of the land. To the right a path leading back to the monastery kitchens, to the left the orchards and beyond the small cemetery.

He made his way along another well trodden path where wheelbarrows had been pushed by monks for centuries. He reached the cemetery wall, went through the gate and straight to the little stone hut in which all the implements were stored.

He took a spade and a shovel and from a shelf a large screwdriver and a hammer in case it proved necessary.

At Brother Martin's graveside he took off his habit, aware that it would limit his movements, aware also that his partially naked body would show up white in the moonlight. But he had to take that risk.

He was surrounded by death and totally defenceless. They could come up behind him, the apparitions, touch him with icy fingers or materialize at any moment anywhere, rise out of the earth, out of the yawning graves, he had no idea what to expect.

He sat down on the earth and made himself listen to the noises of the country night, the cicadas in the fields beyond, the screeching of a small animal, the hollow croak of a frog. He tuned his ears to closer sounds, to the rustle of the breeze in the trees nearby, to another animal, furtive somewhere, a rabbit, a rat?

He could see very clearly now, his eyes completely accustomed to the dark, and he studied Brother Martin's resting place. The mound of fresh earth was soft and would not be too difficult to move, providing he worked slowly and did not exhaust himself.

It was remarkably easy. Once or twice his spade struck a stone and made a clatter which caused him to drop to his haunches and wait to hear if it had disturbed anyone. The night was silent however, and he became more and more confident that no one would interrupt him.

As he got a foot or so down the shifting of the earth became harder and tiredness set in making his pace slower. He sat down to rest, his feet inside the grave, a new mound building up in front of him. He was entering the kingdom of earth animals which he did not like, and he thought of the worm in Signor Sciasia's eye.

After half an hour of further digging and shovelling his spade hit the coffin lid and he worked more quickly though the earth was now sticky and wet, till he could see the wood quite clearly under him. He got out of the grave, lay on the muddy ground and felt along the edge of the lid for the screws. There were twelve, he knew, two at each end and four on either side. He was thankful that he had found the brother-gardener's screwdriver and that it was a good one for the screws came out with some effort.

He discarded the screws, lost them in the earth, then got ready to put his strength into the prizing off of the lid. But there was no need for strength, it lifted off quite easily, releasing an unexpected foul acid odour. It was such a putrefying smell that he had to turn away and take a deep breath before looking down at the shape of the body wrapped in its white shroud.

There were stains on it, body liquids that had started seeping through. For a moment he was not sure he could go on, yet he had to. Putting his hand over his nose, he got down into the grave, knelt on Brother Martin's body, still stiff with rigor mortis, and realized his weight was causing gasses to escape.

It was a fiendish thing to be doing, revolting, and he decided it would be better to pull the dead man out.

He climbed back onto solid ground, placed himself at the top end of the coffin, put his feet firmly on the rim, threaded his hands down the inside of the box and managed to grip the corpse under each armpit.

He pulled. The shrouded body moved. He heaved, five, six times till the stiff cadaver was up and half onto the ground.

Exhausted he knelt next to the figure to catch his breath, then with the very tips of his fingers felt the surface of the damp shroud for the hem, the edge, picked at it and slowly drew the moist material away from the face.

He stared down at the mask of death.

He had expected a smooth skull perhaps, hollows instead of eyes, bones instead of flesh, a hideousness like the metamorphoses he had seen before, but nothing so repellent as the puss oozing from the puffed skin, from between the swollen lips, from the shocked eyes staring sightlessly with an expression of agony as though not believing what had happened to it.

It was a bloated distortion of the human shape. Brother Martin no longer existed, only the chemicals of his body acting unchecked to putrefy.

Afraid that any pressure might cause the jelly skin to slide off the bone, Juan lowered himself cautiously and placed his ear to the forehead to listen.

There was nothing. He had not listened with his ears before, it had been a hard, direct contact.

He moved. He knelt in the grass directly behind the head so that, to him, the awful face was upside down. Then lightly, very lightly he placed his forehead against the soft puffy brow.

For a moment more, there was nothing, then a hollowness, a definite soundlessness, a silence in a vast empty space. He closed his eyes and listened intently and heard the hiss approaching, louder as though gaining speed from an incalculable distance.

It was an awesome sound, like steam escaping from a giant cistern, it was the immensity of the sound that frightened as though he had his ear to the noises of the heavens, of the universe. It was not enclosed, but huge, an immense sound, not enveloping but expanding, a travelling sound on which he himself travelled, then suddenly there was silence again.

"Brother Martin?" He whispered into the night.

"Brother Juan . . . release me . . . Brother Juan . . . release me . . ." The voice was tortured, pleading like a man trapped in a disaster, in agony and about to die. But he was already dead.

"Brother Martin . . . ?" Juan said.

"Juan, help me . . . please help me . . ."

"How? How can I help you?"

Silence. Then he heard the voice again. *"Death is fearful . . . fearful . . ."*

"Where are you?" Juan asked. "Is it purgatory? Are you in hell?"

"Death is unimaginable loneliness. One is all alone, all alone in the skull. All alone in the earth with only the knowledge of insects and the fear of the worms eating one's memory. There is nothing else . . . Death is only a continuance of life's senses but without eyes, without ears, without limbs and without needs . . ."

"What of God?" Juan asked. "What of God and Jesus Christ?"

There was a long silence then a sigh that weighed heavy with suffering, and the voice said in despair, *"There is nothing Juan. Death is waiting for nothing, with no one, for ever."*

"But what of heaven and hell? Of the resurrection, of reincarnation?"

The laugh was hollow, bitter, desperate, weak. *"We have been misled Juan, misled . . . We spend our lives lying to each other to avoid the truth . . ."*

"What is the truth?"

"The truth is that there is no end. We go on as nothing for ever within our skulls, with our memories being eaten away by the slimy creatures of the earth, unless . . ."

"Unless what?"

There was a long pause, so long that Juan thought he had lost him, yet he sensed he was still there. He pressed his head against the dead brow despite the cramps in his legs, the numbness in his fingers, he stayed in the same position pressing hard. "Unless what?" He asked again.

"Thank you for being there Juan, thank you . . ."

"Brother Martin . . . ?"

He had no idea exactly what it was but he felt it as clearly as if a person at the other end of a telephone line had hung up. He knew now that he was alone, kneeling in the earth, slowly becoming aware of his real surroundings. "Brother Martin?" he said into the night, straightening up, holding the head between his hands.

He bent down and pressed his forehead against the cold brow. There was nothing.

He moved to the other end of the coffin, pulled the body by the feet back into the box, arranged the shroud comfortably around the head, then replaced the lid.

He pushed the earth back on top with his hands, then with the spade. He had made a mess around the grave, but by the time he had finished, by the time all the earth was replaced it was as though little had been disturbed.

He had thought that he would leave the cemetery knowing about heaven and hell, about reincarnation, about the wages of sin. He had learned only that there was a sort of life after death, that he could make contact and that this contact did not last.

He was aware that he smelt, that he was filthy with mud, that he was tired so he sat down and looked at the rest of the cemetery. He was surrounded by the dead, some of whom could talk to him, maybe all of them if he could reach them.

Was there a way of speaking to the spirits without the presence of the body, or was the skull all-important? Could one sever a head and carry it around?

He realized he was perspiring, that he was wet with sweat. Perhaps a madness was upon him? Perhaps he had imagined all that he had done. He stood up and walked away, up the path he had come, replaced the spade, the shovel, the screwdriver and hammer in the hut, and made his way towards the kitchen gardens.

He put the tunic over his head, threaded his arms down the sleeves, then stopped, aware that he was not alone.

He held his breath, waited to hear the sound that had disturbed him again, then the figure stepped out of the shadows of a hedge. It was Father Anthony.

"Where have you been?" He asked.

"The cemetery," Juan answered.

"What for?"

"I was talking to Brother Martin . . ."

"How Juan? How did you talk to him?"

"I put my head against his head. It seems to be the necessary way of communication."

"But he is buried."

"I dug him up," Juan said simply.

"Of course," Father Anthony said and, as though addressing a child who had been found sleep walking. "Now I think you should go back to bed."

CHAPTER
— 4 —

There was no lock on the schoolroom door, there were no locks on any of the doors in the monastery, privacy was something that did not exist in the Dominitian Order, for no one had any secrets, supposedly. Father Anthony, however, had devised a way of delaying sudden entry by an unwelcome visitor by simply jamming the door with his own chair, moved to the end of the table to allow the full spreading out of a large map of Classical Greece.

None of this had to be explained, it was obvious as Juan watched Father Anthony first get the map out, then unfold it, then place the chair against the door as though he had pushed it there on getting up.

"Sit in my chair a second, will you?" Father Anthony asked him. He waited till Juan was seated, then crossed the room, bent down by the window and removed a loose skirting tile.

From the cavity behind it he brought out a thick roll of paper held fast by an elastic band. "It's not a very original hiding place, but it works."

He slipped the elastic band off, suggested by a nod of the head that Juan should go back to his own chair and sat down himself in front of the door and started to flatten out the curled pages.

"These are photostat copies of a report which the Abbot holds, and which is also lodged in the archives of the Vatican. It concerns you, and I have decided, not without a great deal of soul searching, to make you aware of its existence." He checked the order of the pages and placed them on his lap. "I am risking a great deal by letting you see this document, for I have been sworn to secrecy, but I personally believe that some members of the Holy Office are not handling the situation as intelligently as they should, so I am putting you in the picture, believing you will honour my trust." He handed the papers over.

"What shall I do with them?" Juan asked, taking the thick roll of paper, not sure whether he should put it under his tunic or not.

"Read them."

"Here?"

"Of course. You can hardly take them to the chapel or the refectory. If anyone comes in, slip them under the map. That is what it is there for. We are studying Odysseus's sea route to Ithaca."

"Of course," Juan said.

He took hold of the wad of strange silky papers which smelt of stale onions and read the title. *Juan Ramirez Montoneros.*

DOCUMENT 1

        ACCIDENT REPORT.

                December 12, 1964.
                11:35 a.m.

Varick/West Houston.
Junction.

Collision involving green Studebaker N.Y. 352 OMY. Black Lincoln N.Y. 698 HTP. White Dodge Van. Pennsylvania 443 XTO. Four eye witnesses (names/addresses attached) confirmed green Studebaker shot lights causing collision. Owner driver Miss Juanita Ramirez Montoneros (22), of 48 East 68th suffered serious injuries and was taken to St Vincent's Hospital. No others were injured. Estimated speed of Studebaker 45 mph.

Sgt Saul Kantz.
17 Precinct. NYPD.

DOCUMENT 2
ST. VINCENT'S HOSPITAL (7th Avenue)
CASUALTY.
PATIENT ACCEPTANCE LIST. December 12th, 1964
12:05 p.m.
JUANITA RAMIREZ MONTONEROS.

Age: 22.
Cranial trauma. Bleeding nose and throat. Temperature normal. Pupils inactive. Respiration irregular. Pulse slow. Blood pressure variable. Evidence of paralysis. X-Ray demonstrated skull fracture and displacement of pineal gland. Superficial cuts to face and hands. *Coma.*

DOCUMENT 3

48 East 68th Street,
New York.
January 10th, 1965.

My Dear Lord Archbishop,

The enclosed gift is a small way of giving thanks to the nuns of Our Saviour for their constant vigilance over my daughter during these very sad times. To know that she is being prayed for is indeed a relief and both my wife and I wish to thank you deeply.

> Yours sincerely,
> Adolfo Ramirez Montoneros

> 48 East 68th Street,
> New York.
> February 6th, 1965.

My Dear Lord Archbishop,

I enclose a further cheque for the church with my grateful thanks for the constant praying and vigilance of your good Sisters. Sadly my daughter, now in her third month of coma, does not appear to be improving. Let us hope your prayers will soon be answered.

> Yours sincerely,
> Adolfo Ramirez Montoneros

> 48 East 68th Street,
> New York.
> April 9th, 1965.

My Dear Lord Archbishop,

I thank you for your letter of April 3rd arranging for Father Dupuis to say Mass for my daughter in the Clinic.

Alas there is still no improvement, nor, I must say thankfully, any worsening of her condition. One must accept that she may remain in her state of unconsciousness for quite some time.

> Yours sincerely,
> Adolfo Ramirez Montoneros

DOCUMENT 4

> The Steiner-Lauder Clinic,
> East 70th Street, New York.
> 3rd June, 1965.

Dear Mr Ramirez Montoneros,

Further to our lengthy conversation this morning I wish to confirm Doctor Brauntmeger's and my own diagnosis of your daughter Juanita's condition. She is in the third month of pregnancy and scan tests have revealed the foetus to be alive and normal.

From our documents, researchers and investigations it appears that she was not pregnant at the time of her entering the clinic from St Vincent's Hospital on 5th January.

I will await your instructions.

Yours sincerely,
Doctor Paul S. Grant

DOCUMENT 5

93-06/110th
Forest Hills, 11375.
June 6.

My Dear Adolfo,

You asked me to confirm what I told you on the phone, and as bluntly. In my opinion Juanita was raped while in a coma in Bedroom 42 of the Steiner-Lauder Clinic during the month of April and you should put the matter immediately in the hands of a lawyer.

Yours,
Bernard

DOCUMENT 6

SHUSTER, WYATT & LOEWS,
MADISON AVENUE, N.Y.
11th July, 1965.

Dear Mr Ramirez Montoneros,

Juanita Ramirez Montoneros

Following your instructions of June 6th, I have myself investigated your daughter's case and would report the following.

According to medical examinations the patient could only have been rendered pregnant between March 1st and March 20th. These twenty days were therefore the only dates with which I concerned myself.

Between 1st and 9th March inclusive and 15th and 20th March inclusive, the patient was watched over constantly by one or more of the Nuns of Our Saviour and at no time, save possibly for a few minutes, was she ever left alone. Enquiries with the said nuns have satisfied me that no negligence could have occurred during this period.

Between 10-14th March, the patient came under the vigilance of Father Dupuis of the Church of St Matthew, and Brother Marcus, a Jesuit monk from the Monastery of Saint Bardolph's, Wisconsin.

Though I am making enquiries about the characters of these reverent men, I feel it highly doubtful that they could be involved, and therefore must now ask you to allow me to investigate your daughter's private life prior to the accident.

Yours sincerely,
Garfield Shuster

SHUSTER, WYATT & LOEWS,
MADISON AVENUE, N.Y.
7th August, 1965.

Dear Mr Ramirez Montoneros,
Juanita Ramirez Montoneros

Further to our lengthy conversation and our meetings on 3rd and 6th August, I would confirm that thorough investigations of your daughter's private life prior to the accident have revealed nothing that could lead us to suspect that she was involved in any way whatsoever with an individual who could have committed the crime.

She had a number of brief platonic relationships with two

young men who are known to your family and whose characters you have vouched for, and up until the day when she was out Christmas shopping at Bloomingdales and was driving downtown to meet a female friend there is no indication that she was involved with anyone unknown.

The Directors of the Steiner-Lauder Clinic have suggested that we now await the birth of the child and have blood tests taken of the male staff which, though not conclusive, could narrow the field down.

Yours sincerely,
Garfield Shuster

Juan looked up. An uneasiness was beginning to grow within him, the total confusion and mess that surrounded his birth was unbelievable. Everything he had been told had been lies. His parents, it was emerging, had not been killed in a plane crash and his father was possibly some unknown freak. He read the next letter which was again from the lawyer.

DOCUMENT 7

SHUSTER, WYATT & LOEWS,
MADISON AVENUE, N.Y.
20th August, 1965.

Dear Mr Ramirez Montoneros,
Juanita Ramirez Montoneros

Further to my telephone call this morning I confirm that my investigators have reported the following on Father Dupuis and Brother Marcus who were with your daughter between March 10th and March 14th.

Father Dupuis is still the incumbent at the Church of St Matthew and has been there since 1958, an honest man in his sixties.

Brother Marcus joined Father Dupuis from the Wisconsin Monastery on 23rd December 1964, with apparent genuine introductory papers, to work at the Church of St Matthew. Bald of appearance, he was said to be extremely amiable, even jovial, and spoke several languages, including Spanish. According to records kept by the Sisters of Our Saviour he took over from Father Dupuis at night and was with the patient for five successive nights. On 15th March he did not return to the Church of St Matthew, leading Father Dupuis to believe that he had gone back to his fold, though he thought it strange that nothing had been said beforehand.

My private investigators, making enquires at the Monastery in Wisconsin, have reported that no such monk was ever known to them, and it must be concluded that Brother Marcus was an imposter, possibly a madman, who unfortunately gained access to your daughter's room.

As it is beyond my province to enter the privacy of the Roman Catholic church, I am writing forthwith to his Emminence Cardinal Mannington for guidance on the matter.

Yours sincerely,
Garfield Shuster

SHUSTER, WYATT & LOEWS,
MADISON AVENUE, N.Y.
3rd September, 1965.

Dear Mr Ramirez Montoneros,
Juanita Ramirez Montoneros

Following an interview granted me by a representative of his Emminence Cardinal Mannington, I am pleased to advise you that they have kindly offered to have one of their people investigate Brother Marcus's infiltration into their "midst."

A certain Father Anthony Pace, based in England and versed in such crimes will be in charge of the enquiries and will be keeping me posted.

Yours sincerely,
Garfield Shuster

Juan looked up again.

So Father Anthony was a detective in priests' clothing, a man who had known the outside world, a man with a far more exciting past than he had imagined. His esteem for him rose but with it he felt a greater sense of insecurity.

The next two letters were an exchange between Father Anthony in England and an Official at the Vatican, dated three years after the investigations had started, over two years after his own birth.

Midham Priory,
Sherborne, Dorset.
7th February, 1968.

Dear Signor Petrucchi,

I am currently engaged in researches on the disappearance of one of our fold, a certain Brother Marcus.

Reading through various files I came across your report on Makar Boleslov, and as his description answers that of Brother Marcus, I would be grateful for further information on this individual.

Yours sincerely,
Father Anthony Pace

Stato Della Citta de Vaticano.
22nd February, 1968.

Dear Father Anthony,

I have pleasure in enclosing a photostat copy of the little information I have on Makar Boleslov, together with a photograph.

Should you unearth further details on his life we would naturally be most interested. The man has remained a complete mystery as far as we are concerned.

> Your obedient servant,
> Giulio Pomona,
> Gendarmerie Pontificia

The next photostat page was a bad reproduction of a man's photograph.

Juan studied it, trying to get a feeling from it. The man was quite bald, and had a particularly large nose, large ears, thick lips under a walrus moustache and heavy black eyebrows, but the most arresting features were his eyes which even in this bad copy stared out from the page with an intensity that was unsettling. Under the photograph was the name Makar Boleslov.

Juan looked up at Father Anthony but the priest was now standing by the window gazing down at whatever was going on below. Juan turned to the next document.

Typed in Italian, it was headed Makar Boleslov and though there was no indication as to whom it was addressed or by whom it had been written, there was the imprint of the official Vatican stamp at the foot of the page.

The sheet attached was an English translation.

DOCUMENT 8
MAKAR BOLESLOV

Presumed born circa 1885, parents unknown, childhood spent in Asia Minor. Joined Midham Priory in 1925. Mention during his novitiate of working in Tibetan Monasteries, the Chitral, Mount Athos, Sufi schools in Persia, Bokhara and Eastern Turkestan over a period of ten years. Disappeared one night in 1933 leaving a nine pointed star symbol deeply chipped in the masonry of his cell.

October 1935. A prospectus entitled *The Institute for the Development of Harmonious Death on Earth* came into the hands of the Gendarmerie Pontificia.

The Prospectus announces the opening of the Institute in Alexandria with the permission of the Egyptian Minister of National Education.

The Institute accepts adults of both sexes, studies to take place in the evenings only, the subjects of study to be rhythmical, medicinal and mental exercises for the development of will, memory, attentive emotion and thinking in the *after life*. Similar institutions are planned to open in Bombay, Kabul, Chicago, Paris and Stockholm.

The head of the Institute labels himself Father *Marcus Boles*. The symbol of the Institute is a nine pointed star within a circle named an "enneagram" purporting to represent the seven planets and seven days of the week (Sun-Sunday, Moon-Monday, Mars-Tuesday, Mercury-Wednesday, Jupiter-Thursday, Venus-Friday, Saturn-Saturday) with two extra esoteric shock points understandable only to the initiated, but believed to represent self induced death on the one hand and re-incarnation on the other.

There was a sound in the passage outside and Father Anthony reacted quickly, motioning Juan to hide the file immediatley, as he crossed the room swiftly so as to be sitting in the chair when the door opened, hitting it.

"Oh, a moment please," Father Anthony said.

He took his time pulling the chair away from the door, making sure the documents were out of sight, and the Abbot came in, pious, all-knowing, wise.

He studied Juan as though over non-existent spectacles, an examination of a strange creature who was in no way dangerous but a curiosity. Then he turned to Father Anthony. "I wonder if you could spare me a moment Father, perhaps in my chambers would be best?"

It was unusual for the Abbot to come himself, he always sent one of his minions, or asked Brother Ignatius who sent one of *his* minions.

"Study the routes, Brother Juan, you will see on Page 189 that Odysseus reached the island of Aeaea when he sent for Elpenor's body from Circe's house."

Juan picked up his pencil and looked pensive. He waited quite a while after both men had left the room before sitting himself down in the chair as though studying the foot of the map. Then he took the file out from its hiding place.

The next document was a letter to His Emminence Cardinal Gregory at the Sacred College of Cardinals written in Father Anthony's familiar beautiful script. The return address was c/o American Express, Madras, India.

Chingleput, 22nd August, 1968.

Your Emminence,

I trust this finds you well.

Following the audience granted me by his Holiness Shri Sharkari, with whom I discussed the ways of the world and the trends towards disbelief, I broached the subject of self-induced death leading to reincarnation, as was requested of me, and have to report an alarming and indeed unsettling "breakthrough." His Holiness mentioned the studies of a lone white man, whom they have been aware of for some time, who travels under various guises of sage, magician and Holy Father. This man, who called himself Makara Bolshev, touched upon Chingleput in 1953, claiming that he could not only remember clearly a previous life on this earth, but knew how he had been reincarnated. He believed that it was his duty to reveal this to the world thus abolishing Christianity and all its doctrines as we know it. He neither saw himself as an evangelist nor a new Messiah, aware that his knowledge would not relieve the sadness in the world, rather increase it as he had proof that there was little meaning to life. We were no more than ants, he said, busily creating anthills for our comfort. There was a necessary pattern of which we were part, but only as moving beings, not as thinking ones. In short he denied God.

He claimed that he had been born of the "near dead", that his mother was a woman who had been in a coma for eleven months following a fall from a horse, that his reincarnation had only been possible because his father's seed had been planted in a woman whose consciousness had left her. The ideal subject, he said, was one in a natural state of coma, not induced by drugs. It was his intention to experiment along this line of belief and if he succeeded in creating a child by this means he would do so. He did not wish to have disciples of his faith, but offspring who, like himself, would inherit the ability to remember previous lives. He said he had once formed a group in Egypt who tried bringing back the dead by the means of rendering comotose women pregnant but that he had eventually been stopped by the authorities following denunciations by members of the families involved. He also claimed that he could predict the day of a man's death after seeing him as a living corpse. We are therefore looking for a psychopath who is intelligent enough to swing the minds of people to his way of thinking, and astute enough to escape the law.

Since it is my belief that Makara Bolshev, Makar Bolslov and Brother Marcus are one and the same person, I truly feel that we need no longer regard him as the responsibility of the church but that the matter should be referred to, possibly, Interpol.

I have the honour to remain, my Lord Cardinal, Your Emminence's devoted and obedient child.

Anthony Pace

CATACOMB

Photostats of three newspaper cuttings followed with their English translations, all dated well before Juan's own birth.

ABC, Madrid, June 1961.
Carmen Hidalgo-Moreno of Jerez de la Frontera, who suffered brain damage following a fall down the steps of her house and became miraculously pregnant during a two-year coma, died while giving birth to a girl. The child was stillborn.

La Nación, Buenos Aires, April 1963.
Surgeons are watching with interest the growth of a child to be born to Pilar Rubio-Gonzales who has been in a coma since the removal of a brain tumour. Señora Rubio-Gonzales has been in a coma for over one year and it is unknown how she became pregnant while in this state, but scientists are studying the possibility that the brain tumour arrested the development of the foetus and that as she gets better the child grows more normally.

La Nación, Buenos Aires, October 1963.
Pilar Rubio-Gonzales gave birth to a dead child and died shortly afterwards herself, never coming out of her unconscious state. A hospital spokesman said the whole business could only be regarded as a freak birth.

There was a note in Father Anthony's handwriting at the foot of this document.
"Both Roman Catholics. It is possible that other such conceptions have occurred with those not of the faith and that the medical authorities terminated the pregnancies.
Are Roman Catholics vulnerable to the experiments of Boleslov due to our attitude toward abortion?"

* * *

The two photostats that followed were of legal documents. One was his mother's death certificate. The other his own birth certificate. Both bore the same date, 19th December 1965. So she had died comotose while giving him birth. He had been born of the near dead.

CHAPTER
— 5 —

Juan wanted to look at himself in a mirror. Not since he had entered the monastery had he ever wanted to see his reflection more. He looked at the next photostat. It was another letter in Father Anthony's handwriting to the Cardinal, but sent from New York before he had been to India investigating Boleslov's past.

> The Delancey Hotel,
> New York.
> 6th March, 1966.

Your Emminence,

I have now had time to study the case of Juanita Ramirez Montoneros and indeed saw the three-month-old boy briefly yesterday.

In my opinion there is a high probability that the child is the result of Boleslov's work, though it is impossible to say whether there is a resemblance. The description of the Brother Marcus who trespassed into the Steiner-Lauder Clinic by deception coincides too much with the likeness we have on record. I would therefore recommend that the boy be watched very carefully, presuming that sooner or later his father will try to contact him, or that the boy will give signs of unnatural behaviour confirming my suspicions.

> I have the honour to remain Your Emminence's devoted and obedient child.
>
> Anthony Pace

Juan heard a noise outside and quickly hid the file under the map, taking up a more studious position.

The door opened, Father Anthony came in alone and smiled at the fact that all looked as innocent as it should.

"The girl's father died this morning," he announced, closing the door.

"What does that mean?" Juan asked.

"From my point of view, or the Vatican's?"

"From both."

"From their point of view it means that you are obviously psychic, that you are something they do not understand and that they may become afraid of a 'leper'."

"From your point of view?"

"It means that I should protect you. I do not see you as an evil entity."

Juan realized he wanted to be alone to have time to think things out. He had learnt so much about himself all at once that he needed to sort things out in his mind. Now the pretty girl's father had died. What could he do about it? "You have been deceiving me, father," he said, pulling the sheaf of documents from under the map.

"Until now I think I have been deceiving myself, believing I could make them see reason. I am, however, in a very difficult position and I truly do not know what to advise."

"What do you *want* of me?" Juan asked.

"It's not what I want, it's what they want: to lock you up and keep you locked up."

"And what do you want of me?"

"I suppose I would like to experiment."

"Experiment?"

"It sounds like vivisection, doesn't it? That is not what I mean. You seem to have an extra sense, you have obviously inherited something from your father, I want to know exactly what."

"From Boleslov?"

"Yes."

"But you have no proof that he is my father?"

"Proof enough."

"All those questions you have asked me over the years—were they towards finding out who I was? Is it me you are interested in, or him?"

"It was him. Now it is you."

"If you found Boleslov, if he turned up one day to claim me, what would you do?"

"I would do nothing, that is I would be fascinated to talk to him, obviously. They, however, would attempt to control him, try to stop him talking."

"Do you think he's alive and around here watching me?"

"I think he is watching you, but not necessarily around here. He knows where you are, that's sure."

"But you have no proof of this either?"

"None whatsoever."

"Why don't you put an advertisement in the paper, ask him to come out, meet me? Let him know somehow that I am developing?" Juan said this lightheartedly but Father Anthony answered him seriously.

"I would. But they won't allow it. They won't allow anything."

Juan watched Father Anthony roll up the photostats, slip the elastic band round them and tuck them back in the hiding place. He then rolled up the maps, replaced the chair in its usual position and sat down.

There were more photostats to be read, more information

in the sheaf of documents he wanted to see, but Juan realized he could not insist on looking at everything in one day.

"Do you trust me?" Father Anthony asked, sitting down opposite Juan.

"I don't have anyone else in the world to trust."

"The Abbot and Brother Ignatius are using you as a pawn in an ambitious game to climb the hierarchy which has absolutely nothing to do with you. You are of interest to certain people in the Vatican, in that they fear what Boleslov could do to upset world credulity in the Christian credo if, let us say, he appeared on television and told them that you existed and that both of you could foresee people's deaths. It would be most unsettling and they have no means of stopping him except by holding you."

"So they want me as a hostage?"

"In its simplest terms, yes. Brother Ignatius, together with three Cardinals, wishes to keep you silent and servile within the Order. The Abbot, with the other Cardinals, wishes to develop you, educate you, so that maybe one day you could be of use to the church. The main objection to that is your possible rise to a position of too much authority. The whole subject is to be debated at a council."

"Where do you stand?" Juan asked.

"At present I am your spokesman and know that I hold sway one way or the other. I am therefore being charmed by the Abbot and by Brother Ignatius, for whoever wins this battle will no doubt leave the monastery and get an appointment within the Vatican."

For the first time Juan was seeing Father Anthony in a different light. There was a look in his eyes, an eagerness, which he had never observed. All these men, enclosed in the narrowest of monastic worlds, were ambitious. If he was a pawn in a game between the Abbot and Brother Ignatius, surely Father Anthony was also playing the game, and he was just as much a pawn to him.

In reality Father Anthony was telling him, though he might not realize it, that he was going to back the Abbot so that he would go to the Vatican himself.

As much as he had travelled, as learned as he was, Juan felt there was a difference between cleverness and intelligence. Father Anthony was an academic, but he could only work within his limited territory, he apparently could not see that little Juan had a mind of his own and might pursue his own ambitions as well as Father Anthony's experiments.

"You must do as you think best, Father," Juan said, dutifully. "As I said, you are the only person in the world I can trust."

And as he said this, he realized that of course it was no longer true. By handing him the documents Father Anthony had also handed him someone else in the world he could turn to: Makar Boleslov, his own father. Somewhere out there someone cared for him more than anyone else, someone of his own blood.

Somewhere out there a man was waiting for a sign, so his loyalty was suddenly no longer to Father Anthony or Brother Ignatius, it was no longer to the Monastery of Saint Dominitian, nor to the Roman Catholic Church, nor to the Vatican, it was to Boleslov, to his own father who knew so much more about life and death than anyone else.

He, Juan Ramirez-Montoneros-Boleslov was now what he had always wanted to be, what he had always dreamt of being: a man of substance, a man with a duty, a man with a mission.

"What are you thinking about?" Father Anthony asked, cutting into his silence.

"I was thinking that it would be pleasant to leave this monastery for the Vatican," Juan said diplomatically.

"I think it would be too," Father Anthony agreed.

"When is the council meeting?"

"Next week. The sessions start on Tuesday."

"And the Pope will accept the decision of the council?"

"In all probability, yes."

"Whether I am to be incarcerated here for life or developed as a human being within the celestial palace?"

"Yes."

"Perhaps I should escape while I have the chance?"

"I wouldn't try. Unknown to most of us, the Roman Catholic church, in all its magnificence, has its own security agency."

The hardest thing of all was to stop smiling, to stop looking pleased, looking happy. The secret deep within him was so unbelievably marvellous that he wanted to jump for joy, but young monks in the service of Jesus Christ and the Virgin Mary at the Monastery of Trasimeno were not allowed to jump for joy, or jump at all for that matter.

It was like having had a heavy iron dustbin lid lifted off his head. He had popped out of the bin, looked around, decided he could get out, had to get out, and now it was just a matter of how and when.

He now had time to think because he no longer had to pray. As he knelt down in the chapel for vespers with all the other brothers he realized he did not *have* to pray. All these years he had dutifully knelt down and mumbled his Ave Marias, his Our Fathers, had sung the Canticles and felt devout, had believed he was doing some good. But suddenly Father Anthony had shown him the file. Why? Because Juan would help him up the celestial ladder. Without Juan of the unknown powers Father Anthony would probably either remain in the monastery all his life or be sent back to his wet and damp England to be forgotten by the world.

Juan could trust no one, except his magical, saintly father, the ogre Boleslov. And there was more to learn, he had only seen half of the documents.

After vespers he would be able to sneak up to the schoolroom, he would not be missed during the half hour or so before supper. When the service ended he slowly made his way there.

He went in, closed the door and went straight to the loose skirting tile.

The evening sun was going down and a bright pink light was coming through the window. Should someone come in, all he had to do was pretend he was studying a book. If Father Anthony came in, then he would just admit to what he was doing.

He took out the documents, replaced the tile, slipped the elastic band off the photostats and leafed through them till he found the section he had not yet read.

It started with a letter dated 1974, when he was eight, from Father Anthony in Argentina to a Cardinal in Rome.

> San Nicolas de la Villa,
> Buenos Aires.
> July 4th, 1974.

Your Emminence,

I have to report that on June 30th Juan Ramirez-Montoneros suffered what can best be termed a hallucination. He claimed to have seen his own grandfather as a ghost, a skeletal figure walking on the balcony of the house overlooking the garden where he was playing.

Adolfo Ramirez-Montoneros died the following day. I leave you to deduce whether there is any connection between the death and his grandson's hallucination.

The boy has since recovered from his obviously unsettling experience but has entered an uncharacteristic mood, seeking solitude. I spoke to him myself and he simply stated that he saw his grandfather as a dead man walking, his skull covered with grey skin tissue. The apparition beckoned, and seemed to "stare down at him."

> I remain, your Emminence,
> yours faithfully,
> Father Anthony Pace

Juan looked across the schoolroom, then out of the window. He had no recollection of ever seeing Father Anthony before coming to the monastery.

The next letter was from New York and concerned his seeing the apparition of Magdalena, and a meeting with Father Brian of St Anselm's College.

The next letter was also from New York.

> The Gorham Hotel,
> 136 West 55th Street,
> New York.
> 6th January, 1977.

Your Emminence,

Juan's grandmother died yesterday at noon. In the evening, when he returned from school he went to her room and a few minutes later was heard to scream uncontrollably.

On entering the room Juan was found cowering in a corner and his grandmother's body, originally lying on the bed, was on the floor as though disembowelled.

He swore that he had not touched her but that the corpse had sat up and torn itself with its own hands.

I understand that both his aunt and uncle are seeking advice from their family doctor and are considering psychiatry. I would therefore suggest that the time is right for them to be approached with the idea that he should enter Saint Luke's. From there he could more naturally be moved to a monastery where he could be put under constant but discreet surveillance.

I would mention that he is a particularly bright boy and is known for his clear voice and musical ear. St Luke's has a reputation as a "musical" school so that the boy would not become suspicious.

> Your obedient servant,
> Father Anthony Pace

So what of the exam he had had to take to get accepted into the Dominitian Order, and the fuss that had been made, and the feverish time he had had with his uncle, who had lectured him on the joys of becoming a priest, of the honour for his family, his father's memory, his mother's. Had his aunt and uncle been duped too, or were they partisan to this deceit. The church, in all its glory, had been evil!

There had been so many lies! And Father Anthony, the biggest liar of all, posing as his tutor. He was no tutor at all, but a spy, a Vatican spy keeping an eye on the possible offspring of . . . what? The devil incarnate?

He flicked the pages back to the photograph of Makar Boleslov. Was this man his father? The man who had raped his unconscious mother?

Was he watching too? Did he, Juan Boleslov, have brothers and sisters who suffered similar experiences with the dead?

The pages that followed were photostats of every one of his school reports, both from Buenos Aires and New York. He looked at the last letter in the file.

> The Monastery of Saint Dominitian,
> Trasimeno.
> 19th September, 1978.

Your Emminence,

I am pleased to report that our new Brother Juan has settled in nicely amongst us and that the Abbot regards his youthfulness as beneficial to the community. After two months he is showing genuine interest in the classics and has embraced the Faith with commendable enthusiasm.

Could it be that his inherited evil strain is dying within these sacred walls? We must continue to pray that it is so.

Your obedient servant,
Father Anthony Pace

The bell tolled for supper. Quickly he rolled up the documents, slipped on the elastic band and replaced them behind the skirting tile.

He left the schoolroom unseen, and joined his worthy brothers in the cloisters on their hungry way to the refectory.

Tonight it was cold beans and tomato salad.

He now understood why they had never taught him Italian; it would make it so much more difficult for him to escape.

One journey in an enclosed car to a hospital in three years protected by two of them! He had been blind.

But how would he escape, then? He had no clothes. They had even taken care of that easily enough, he had outgrown those he had worn on coming in. And money? A prisoner in a prison without bars.

Strange that he had never seriously thought of escaping until now. But then he had never seen himself as captive.

He would have to escape at night of course, which would not be too difficult. He had rehearsed it by going to the cemetery, had he not? He had the feeling before, the inner knowledge that more was expected of him by someone, that he might become a person to be reckoned with. He had thought the someone was God. Well, God was a man called Boleslov. God the Father Boleslov.

He had been denied both parents by a lie then handed

an incredible father on a silver platter. They thought he was the devil's son!

In their limited superstitious minds they thought he was the devil's son. At least Father Anthony was more logical, but then if you believed in the Virgin Mary, in the Immaculate Conception, in the resurrection of a human being, in ghosts virtually, why not the devil, with a tail and horns and breathing fire?

Boleslov the Devil.

He might have inherited supernatural powers then, perhaps he could perform miracles, stand in front of the monastery wall and blow it down, find the strength of Samson and push the whole lot over.

He would escape.

He would just go and hope that Boleslov came out of hiding to help him, even if it was only with a ham sandwich when he was hungry.

The evening rituals followed one after another, then eventually it was time for sleep.

Alone, he knelt down by his bed and said his prayers. Habit, routine. But the prayer was different.

"If you exist, dear God, and are listening to me and can help me, then help me understand what is happening to me and why, and help me escape."

He awoke as dawn was breaking. He got up, put on his sandals and tunic, and left his cell. There was no one around. He went up to the huge portals, pulled back the massive bolt on the inner door, opened it and stepped out into the pink morning world.

He took long confident steps, putting distance between himself and holy incarceration, then heard a bell ringing. Was it five o'clock already, or an alarm? He quickened his strides heading for the road leading to Monte di Trasimeno.

He became aware of a mechanical sound behind him.

Turning cautiously he saw the lights of a vehicle coming down the road at a fair speed. It was an old van, a farmer's van no doubt taking merchandise to the market.

He gave a friendly wave as the van drove past, and to his surprise it stopped.

"Trasimeno?" an enthusiastic face enquired.

He got in. He did not have to talk, no one would expect a monk from the monastery to talk. He was an accepted mute.

Unlike the comfortable limousine ride he had had with the Abbot and Father Anthony, this was a bumpy experience. The peasant, for that is what he was, wore an old straw hat, a grey shirt, grey trousers and smelt of onions. He had an unlit cigarette stuck in the corner of his mouth and he talked, non stop, about goodness knows what.

The van bumped its way along the road till it came to a junction. The signpost indicated Arezzo or Perugia. The driver stuck out his hand because his indicator didn't work, and turned right.

Now there were people on the road, people on bicycles, a grey car speeding past followed by a motorbike chasing it, the noises were exhilarating. A woman on a moped, two men walking, a girl, two or three girls now as they came closer to the town. He would spend his whole day just looking at people, at the faces, listening to their voices.

The van suddenly swerved and stopped. For a moment Juan thought they had hit someone, but it was just the farmer parking in a free space near the market.

He put out his hand to shake Juan goodbye, and Juan instinctively made the sign of the cross in way of blessing him, and the man, grateful, crossed himself afterwards. What right had Juan had to do that? None at all, but this was the country to be in if you were dressed as a monk.

Juan did not know where the station was, but it would

not be difficult to find it. There were more people around than he had expected this early, which was good, for he got lost in the crowd as he walked, carefree, looking at the shops. There were not many but they had new things in the windows which were pleasing. The radio shop with its small portable television sets and transistor radios. He would want one of those. Pocket calculators, a red and white iron of such steamlined design, colourful pots and pans.

He hurried. He had to bear in mind that there might be someone from the monastery in the village who would spot him, or that Father Anthony might have guessed he had escaped and would be heading for the railway station.

He would have to change clothes. But how? How did a young monk walk into a shop and ask for a change of clothing without money? He was not going to steal. Whom did he know in the whole wide world who could help him?

He thought of the girl whose father had died. She spoke English, would recognize him perhaps, would be sympathetic. He would go to Rome and find her, such a gentle person was bound to help him if he told her his whole story.

A rumbling to his left made him turn around. It was a train. Ahead he saw the level crossing and the station. He started running. A train! It didn't matter what direction. If he could catch the train as though he were late for it, crash through the ticket barrier, they wouldn't stop him. He made a quick sign of the cross and sprinted.

He did not look to left or right, he dashed. In through the double doors, across a wide airy hallway, onto the platform, the train was about to move off, all the doors were closed. He grabbed hold of the brass handrail, pulled himself up on the steps and the door opened for him.

A railway official in uniform helped him up and he smiled thankfully. The man said something insignificant and made way for him. He smiled at the man again and the man smiled back with his eyes, a strange look, the same strange look that Brother Martin had always given him, the same look that Kidson the Head Prefect at St Anselm's had given him till he had allowed him to do things to him one night in the bathroom next to the dormitory.

It was a weapon in his life he had never thought of using, his looks. If things came to the worst, he realized, a young boy dressed as a monk had its attractions for certain people.

He sat down on the hard green leather seat of the first compartment, thankful that he had made it.

What would he do when asked for a ticket was the next problem. He would pretend ignorance, act dumb, play with his eyes and make the sign of the cross. At least there were no other monks or priests or nuns around, just one soldier, one old man and the inevitable grandmother knitting baby socks.

He started to relax. The train gathered speed, then slowed down and stopped at Chiusi. At Orvieto the station announcer told passengers that it was the express train, next stop Roma. He was on his way to Rome, the big city where he would be able to lose his pursuers if there were any.

It was so hot, even this early in the morning, that everyone was fanning themselves, or falling asleep. He was not sleepy, he was too excited. He stood up and went to the corridor and leaned his head out of the window. The hot fresh air was marvellous. He watched the cars on the motorway which ran parallel to the train, the river Tiber in between. El Tiverne. He wouldn't mind diving into that.

He went back to sit down as the uniformed man came to collect the tickets. There were more people in the compartment now, a business man in black with a briefcase, a rich woman tourist with many rings on her fat fingers, a nervous girl student with glasses which kept slipping down her nose. The ticket collector held out his hand. Juan looked up at him as innocently as he knew how.

"Dove va lei, Roma?" The collector asked.

"I will pay," the rich woman said, *"Yo pago . . . !"* She fished for money in the depth of a dark blue crocodile handbag. *"Yo hablo español, pero no Italiano!"* She explained to the uninterested company present. She refused to give the notes that came out of her bag directly to the collector, but handed them to Juan, who paid the man, and the man handed him the change which he tried to give to the woman.

She refused. "No, keep it, give it to the poor or whatever you think best."

He looked at the money in his hand. Two thousand lire, the equivalent of two dollars he knew. It would be very useful.

He acknowledged thanks, mimicked gratefulness and made the sign of the cross which embarrassed her. He had not been aware till then that the monks had taught him one thing with their vows of silence: the art of mime. He was now a trained actor.

Eventually the countryside was lost to houses and buildings which became taller, higher, till suddenly they were in Rome itself.

At the station he was overwhelmed by the number of people about, at the rush, the panic, the pace at which they moved.

His astonishment must have been evident for the rich lady smiled at him sympathetically. *"Mucha gentes, siempre* in a hurry," she said, in a mixture of Spanish and American.

He smiled agreement, taking her smart leather suitcase down from the rack for her and then onto the platform.

As she said *"Grazie"* and smiled, her pale powdered skin, bluish mascara and bright pink lipstick changed colour quite suddenly to shades of yellow and the hollows of her eyes showed through the transparent eyelids and the bright pink gums of her dentures and the whiteness of her false teeth looked fearful against the grey palor of her jaw bones.

He looked at her hands expecting to see spindly bones, but she was wearing white gloves. When he looked up again her face had resumed the appearance of the living.

"You are very young to lock yourself away from life," she said, "*La vida* is so precious, you should get out in the world and enjoy it! That's what I am doing."

And he realized that she had absolutely no idea, but no idea at all that very soon, terribly soon, she would be dead, and that he was the only person in the world who knew it.

Unless his father was somewhere in the mad chaos of people around, watching.

CHAPTER
— 6 —

So he could stare death in the face.

Not only could he do that, but he could do it without being frightened. He was getting used to it. The eighth apparition, the eighth vision. It shocked, of course, it took him by surprise and unsettled him for a while, but he no longer felt sick, no longer felt the need to run to someone to tell them.

He could see the dead before they died, he could talk to them after they died: a sixth sense that seemed to have little purpose unless it was a stepping stone, a form of training for what was to come. Maybe he was not only a novice of the church, maybe he was a novice of the world beyond.

The Vatican had its own secret agency, Father Anthony had said. Would they be waiting for him here? Would the Abbot have put out a call for help so soon, would Father Anthony have advised him to do so? He doubted it. Time for the moment was on his side but he would have to get a change of clothing.

All he needed was a pair of jeans and a T-shirt, his Saint Dominitian sandals weren't that unique, they would not exactly give him away.

He was out in the big wide world now, and it was huge.

The Piazza del Cinquecento was throbbing with life. He had no idea where to go. He had a vague recollection of ancient Rome with its Arch of Titus, the Palatine Hill, but this bustling place of racing taxis, Vespas, screeching tyres and mad, mad rushing was totally foreign.

He headed down one side of the terminal, a long road of cobblestones with little on either side but warehouses. No shops, few people.

A priest came round the corner, black cassock, black biretta.

He froze. It was like being a criminal and seeing the police. And Rome would be full of them. He quickened his steps, head down, pretended he was into the rosary. The priest went by on the other side, no Samaritan he.

But he was doing it wrong. Completely wrong. If they were looking for him they would not be looking for him around the Vatican. An escaped convict would not hang around other prisons. What he had to do, especially until he could discard his habit, was hang around where he would be least noticed.

He took a left and a left again, was back in the Piazza del Cinquecento and now in the Via Cavour where there were shops in abundance, shoe shops, clothes shops, surplus clothing stores. Jeans at 30,000 lire, T-shirts 10,000 lire. How could he ever find the money to buy those? Two thousand lire would buy him a meal, just, a pizza which he would soon need, maybe a Coca-Cola.

He hadn't had a Coca-Cola for three years!

Ahead he could see the high monument of the Piazza di Venezia. He walked on. Down to the Via del Corso with its fashionable shops. Hundreds of people were milling around, there were so many ways in which they dressed. He could not have been found if he had been wearing a bright pink suit.

Saldi one shop announced, with "sale" baskets of clothing out on the pavement. Cotton shirts for 1,000 lire. But no trousers. Who would have thought that he would one day be crying out for a pair of cheap trousers? Stealing a pair wouldn't be easy. And then what if he were caught? The Vatican police would be called and there would be an excuse for the Cardinal to incarcerate him for life.

He turned into a side street where there were even more people, and for a good reason: the fountain, the famous Trevi fountain, was crammed in a small piazza with thousands of young people watching the water tumble down over the Bernini sculptures. He knew the Trevi fountain well, had seen it so often in picture books. So there it was, scarred, dirty, Fanta bottles and cans floating in the clear water, the marble stained with rust, a disappointment in a way.

Two silly tourists stood on the edge of the pool and threw coins into the water for luck.

He walked slowly towards the tourists and shyly put out his hand. They both looked at him uncertainly for a moment, then dug into their leather handbags and placed notes in his palm.

He made the sign of the cross and walked on. A thousand lire. One dollar. He would have to work at it much harder.

He moved on, up a pedestrian precinct, and found himself facing the famous Spanish Steps with the church of San Trinita dei Monte at the top. He had been made to study pictures of all the famous churches in Rome at St Anselm's. So everything eventually became useful.

Among the tourists he noticed two small children, thin, with dirty brown legs, dressed in ragged clothes. The older boy was eight maybe, the younger girl six, their little faces were drawn, their hair matted with dust—full of fleas no doubt. They moved from one group of people to another, their hands out, cupped, begging with no success. Their eyes stared at the older, healthier faces. They said nothing, just pleaded with their eyes.

But they were too impatient, gave up too quickly, the nuisance value was nil and the majority of people managed to avoid looking at them.

The boy turned and saw Juan. Would they beg from him now? They came, slowly, stopping on the way with no success. Were they genuinely starving or working for their drunken parents, as reputation had it? The little boy now came right up to him. One of his teeth was missing, his face looked as if it hadn't been washed for weeks. He looked at Juan and shrugged his shoulders, as much as to say that they were not paying out today.

Was it customary for such orphans to be taken in by monks and given a meal? How could he explain to them what he really was?

He put a hand naturally on each of their shoulders and like the holy picture of Saint Nicolas he walked with them away from the steps and down another side street.

They walked for quite a while, the children apparently finding comfort in his presence, believing in the security of the image this man of God promoted by the very habit he was wearing.

It was getting near lunchtime now, smells of food drifted from the restaurants they passed, the forgotten pangs of hunger started again.

At a trattoria, early customers filled their mouths with lengths of pasta and glasses of dewy white wine. In a corner sat a very old couple, the woman with blue rinsed hair, her wrists heavy with gold jewellery, the man opposite her pale as the napkin he had tucked into his oversized collar, sipping soup, dribbling some.

He looked at Juan, looked at the children, and the woman

expressed disgust that such people should be allowed on the streets let alone allowed to live and offend her eyes.

Then Juan saw the metamorphosis beginning, the man's bald head turning grey, the skull showing through translucent skin, the orbits becoming defined, the eyes disappearing altogether, the nose reduced to small black wet holes, the teeth yellow, stuck loosely in the jaw, the same doleful expression retained somehow with no features, the long spindly white bones holding the spoon.

A skeleton eating at a restaurant. He had so few hours to live, this man.

Juan made an effort, closed this eyes to get rid of the image, and when he opened them the man slowly came back to life. As Juan stared he realized the man was arguing with the woman. She was protesting as he was digging into his jacket pocket, bringing out a beautiful polished leather wallet and pulling out notes. Not one or two notes but several.

Instinctively Juan pushed the two children forward towards the old man who was holding out the notes. The boy cautiously made his way through the tables and took the money, acknowledging thanks with a nod of the head. A waiter came out to chase him off viciously with his napkin as though flicking away a fly, then he saw Juan and hesitated.

Did Juan appear like a messenger of death to the old man? Was he frightening? He put his arms round his children and turned them away and walked slowly on up the street watching the boy counting the money. Twenty thousand lire. Twenty dollars!

The little boy kissed and hugged his sister who looked amazed. They had never seen so much money in their lives. Then the boy, without hesitation, looked up and handed half to Juan. The generosity was natural, they had worked as a team, without him they could never have earned that much.

Juan took his share and led them straight to a pizzeria where he ordered a huge pizza and several large glasses of Coke.

The three ate greedily, heartily, and when they had finished the little boy looked up at the price card on the wall and calculated how much the meal had cost and counted out so many thousand lire. Juan refused, indicating that the treat was on him. He paid and left with the equivalent of six dollars still in hand.

It was when he was trying on a pair of trousers in front of the cubicle mirror that he felt the sensation of not belonging to himself. It was not new, it had happened before, but he had forgotten.

He had gone into the store where he had seen the T-shirts and found some really cheap trousers his size. He was staring at this youth he hardly knew, making faces, pulling out his tongue, when he felt himself receding, shrinking, departing from his physical shape, yet not. The sensation was one of being pulled back into the past, and as he stared at his feet he felt himself being lifted and placed horizontally on a hard flat surface, tied down so that he could barely see his white legs chained at the ankles to a diabolical wooden pole.

How old was he, and where and when? Hooded men were turning the pole and the pain in his hip joints and his knees was incredible. Blood oozed out of the chains around his blueish feet, his wrists and arms at the elbows were in agony too.

The images of the past came to him when he looked at himself in a mirror. That is why he had not had recurrences of them for so long. In the New York bathroom, he remembered, his aunt's bathroom with the ceiling-to-floor mirror, he had had the most memorable experience, standing there nude after having a bath, drying himself with the huge white towel.

The whiteness had dazzled him and he had entered a memory of medieval splendour, a new church, a new cathedral with sparkling white marble, and had felt the coldness beneath his bare feet because he had been naked yet surrounded by the clothed? He had been walking away from the altar and out into the open, and there had been crowds waiting for him and others, and he had been burnt alive, had he not? Burnt at the stake in a bright white square crowded with black and brown clothed people.

A martyr reincarnated as a novice monk. Would he end up being burnt again?

He came out of it, aware that the memory had lasted but a few intense seconds. He draped his brown tunic over his arm and went to pay at the desk where the cashier was so busy that he did not even look up.

Juan requested a carrier for the tunic. The man took the habit from him, thrust it in a plastic bag. Who cared about young monks discarding the cloth? Next!

Juan walked out into the street deliriously happy. He was a normal human being again, one of the crowd, one *in* the crowd indistinguishable from others.

Where should he start the search for his father? Could the dead tell him? Were they his friends? He started to run down the street for no reason at all and in no particular direction. He had not run for so long.

He passed a chemist's and stopped. In the window was a display of electric shavers. He would need one of those soon, and he would buy one. He would do so many things. He sidestepped people, bumped into them, got hooted at by cars driving close to the kerb.

In an alley-way he passed a pile of rubbish. With glee he swung the plastic bag over his head, let go and watched it land on the dump. So much for the Order of St Dominitian.

He walked across Rome non-stop till it got dark. He looked up, at the buildings, the people, the traffic, listened to the intense noise, stared at the posters, the pictures outside the cinemas, he imbibed life again to the full.

Sooner or later he would have to eat again, but now his time was for savouring his new-found freedom.

He sat down by the Trevi fountain again, having gone in a full vast circle. The night crowds were seeking the cooler air by the water and there were people of every age, every colour, smoking, chewing, licking ice creams. A well-dressed middle aged man sat down next to him at the fountain edge and asked him if he was alone, if he was Italian. Could it be his father? He did not look much like Boleslov.

"I am American, and yes I am alone," Juan said.

"Have you eaten yet? I have not, and wondered whether you would like to join me?"

A Scandinavian pederast. Juan accepted the invitation knowing full well what would be expected of him. The look in the eyes was there.

The Scandinavian took him to a small restaurant, up some wooden steps in a narrow lane. There were tables for two, romantic lampshades, pink table cloths. Juan had a three course meal, fish, meat, ice cream, talked about New York, told his host he was a student, played the complete innocent, deliberately misunderstanding any allusions to what might happen after they had eaten. He gave the man the slip so simply that he felt quite bad. He had no father confessor now to alleviate the guilt.

He walked some more and reached the Colisseum, went round it and lay down on an area of dry grass in the shadow of the ruins. The night was so warm others were sleeping out. He rolled over on his stomach, lay his head on his folded arms and fell asleep.

For five days he managed to exist on next to nothing, stealing food once, begging twice and being invited twice, once by another homosexual, the other time by a group of American students who slept out in the Villa Borghese Gardens and had more food than they could eat.

It was when they suggested that he should join them on their next lap around Europe, and he declined, that he realized that though he had allowed himself a few days of unfettered freedom, deep down he knew he had a duty to perform.

The duty was to the dead.

A fear started to possess him on his sixth day alone. He had spent a happy early morning helping the students to pack and to purchase food for the journey, and when he had waved them goodbye on their way south to Naples, he had sensed an emptiness in his life, a loneliness which was quite unbearable, so much so that he had deliberately walked to St Peter's and stared up at the Basilica and wondered whether, after all, the priesthood was not his true vocation.

As he looked at the architectural splendour of the Piazza and the famous dome itself he knew he could belong there. He could live in that world of religious magnificence if he wished. All he had to do was report back to the monastery, humbly confess, work his way into the Abbot's or Brother Ignatius's good books and take his vows. Then in time, in ten years, twenty years, he might become a priest as so many others did, hoping to serve God under Michelangelo's dome.

He went up the stairs and in, stared up and around at the glory and, for an hour or so, listened to the delightful silence, the whispering tourists awed, not so much by God's presence, as by the sheer weight of beauty that surrounded them.

He wandered away from the Basilica and joined the crowd of sightseers queueing to get into the Vatican museums.

He dodged the ticket collector and was in free, like so many others, up the majestic steps into the countless rooms and galleries. While following the signs to the Sistine chapel, he found himself in corridors filled with Egyptian mummies. He had not expected this and found it unsettling after the Renaissance surroundings, but he stopped to study a sarcophagus, and a mummy case of carved wood painted delicately in pale reds and blues.

It was not unfamiliar. And as he gazed at it he clearly saw in his mind his own hands working with rolls of linen, dripping them in jars of myrrh and olive oil, honey and cedar oil. Between layers of bandages he layed precious stones, bracelets, necklaces, pendants and scarabs.

Had he read of this—the removal of the eyes to substitute jewels—or was it memory? Had he read of the jelly-like touch when he removed those eyes, the initial nervous attempt with the fingers not to damage the cornea, and then the inevitable gouging out with the hook, and the horror of the spurting blood.

He hadn't read of that.

It was a memory from a previous life! He hadn't read of the flies that swarmed around him as he drew the sickly brains out of the nostrils, nor had he read of the smell he could now remember, the repugnant odour that had haunted him till his death. His death? But when?

He was alone in the room and a uniformed attendant was discreetly showing the way out to others in the corridor beyond. 2 p.m. Closing time.

He left, quickly, thankful that the exhibits could no longer remind him of his possible past.

Outside in the heat he walked down the Via della Conciliazone, happy to be surrounded by traffic noises.

If he had lived before in ancient Egypt, then he had again been connected with the dead. And where on earth could he go in Rome where history was not connected with the dead. History was *about* the dead. Should he have gone with the travelling students then, been more adventurous, started at least on a possible way back to America, to his roots, to his father?

Maybe his father was dead. How would he ever know? If the great Vatican detective, his tutor, had been unable to find out, how could he?

Another day of hunger then? Of begging, of deceit to survive. He leaned on a bridge and looked down at the green waters of the Tiber. Should he jump and end it all in this present, enter the next phase, live in his skull till it perished with the buffeting of the waters? His body would be fished out and put on a mortuary slab, then buried next to Brother Martin with obsequies.

He didn't want that. To think that in this vast city of some three million people he knew no one, not one person, unless he could count the girl with the grey-blue eyes in the hospital with her dying father, as a friend.

Where would the old man have been buried? Where would she go, like the good girl that she was, to put flowers on the new grave? The Campo Verano cemetery. He had heard of its elaborate tombs, its rococo homages to the dead.

It was somewhere to go. Perhaps there would be a body there waiting for him to communicate with it. Was he going truly mad to have such thoughts? Was all this necromancy evidence of an unbalanced mind?

*   *   *

He reached the wide open space in front of the cemetery in the late afternoon. In front of the imposing entrance gate there were huge flower stalls with banks of bright colours and foliage all freshly watered.

The cemetery itself was enormous, a park for the dead with wide avenues of gravel between line upon line of tombs and monuments. He would walk around, cross and recross till he found the fresh mounds with recent wreaths. He followed a small group of people carrying bunches of fresh flowers who led him to an area where there was still spare ground for the dead to come. There were several new graves, seven he counted altogether, some with flowers, some with a few, some without, one with a small vase and a small bunch of roses in it. This, he decided, was the one. Instinct, intuition, he didn't know, but he felt that this was the grave of the old man, and he looked around hoping that the girl might turn up out of the blue.

Until now he had not seriously thought of ever meeting up with her, it was too ludicrous an idea, but certain that he was at her father's graveside, the remote possibility of seeing her again seemed to become more and more likely, and he walked up the steep incline to sit on a bench in the shade of the abundant cypress trees.

After an hour or so of peaceful contemplation, watching the mourners sadly staring at the memories of their beloved departed, he decided to leave, and as he stood up he saw her coming from the direction of a little chapel, a bunch of roses in her hand.

Anyone could have guessed it of course, it had been simple deduction. He must not on any account start believing in himself as a gifted psychic.

He approached her, circled the new grave and stood close by. She looked up, smiled, then altered the smile to a frown, puzzled but not frightened.

He was a fraction taller than her, two, three inches maybe, stronger, but they were the same build, the same mould. She carried a black plastic shopping bag, her hands were long, her fingers thin with delicate nails.

"I'm sorry to disturb you at peace with your father," he said, "We met at the hospital, St Cecilia's, a short time ago."

"Yes. I remember you now. You came from the Monastery at Trasimeno with the Abbot and Father Anthony just before my father died."

She knew them then.

"I remember you particularly because my father said something rather curious about you. He said, 'He knows I am going to die very soon.' And he died the following day."

It was a confirmation. People saw him as an angel of death.

"What are you doing here?" she asked.

"Nothing special. I have left the monastery."

"Oh." She seemed shocked.

He had not, of course, considered that she might be extremely pious, devoted to the church. She had seemed to fear the Abbot and have a sympathy for Father Anthony, had shown signs of a rebelliousness against authority. Maybe her father's death had changed her. Was she reliant on the church perhaps?

"Why have you left the order?" she asked, kneeling down to change the roses in the vase on the grave.

What could he tell her? He had come so unprepared for this, he had not considered alternatives at all. "A misunderstanding which I don't . . . understand . . ." he said awkwardly. He realized he was nervous in her presence. He had never spoken to a girl before, not alone, not for three years.

"Why don't you tell me about it? Are you doing anything special? I have to go back to the centre, I'm taking a bus from just outside the gates." Satisfied that the roses were well arranged, she then led the way back to the main gate, Juan following her a step or two behind.

He stood in the bus queue with her and others who had been to the cemetery, widows with red eyes, sad men, a lost tourist scanning a large map not knowing where he was.

She was the first to offer help of course. He was German, but spoke some English. He had got the Colisseum mixed up with the Circus Maximus, and the Protestant cemetery confused with the Campo Verano. She sorted it all out for him, then turned her attention to Juan.

"I don't know your name," she said.

"Juan. Juan Ramirez Montoneros. I was called Brother Juan."

"How did you get those clothes?"

He told her and she was amused.

"You seem to think of yourself as an escaped prisoner."

"That's how I feel. I think they may be looking for me."

"Oh, I doubt it. If you want to leave surely you just do so. What are you going to do now?"

"I want to get out of Italy. I want to go home to America, I suppose."

"You suppose?"

The bus came and they clambered on. It was not too crowded and he sat down next to her on one of the front seats.

"I don't know how to go about it," he said, "I have no money."

"Why don't you go to the American consul and ask advice there? Tell them of your predicament, if you really have one, and if not go and see the Abbot. Surely he will understand and help you. Did you arrive at the monastery with nothing at all?"

"I don't know. I was sent straight from school. I know nothing of my true circumstances."

She smiled at him. She was really quite beautiful when she smiled.

"Perhaps I'd like to stay in Rome," he said, smiling back. "With you."

"For an American you seem to have learnt the ways of Italian charm very quickly. Surely not in the monastery?"

"I am of Spanish descent," he said, "I was born in Buenos Aires."

"Oh . . . That explains it then." She unexpectedly put her hand on his.

"What is *your* name?" He asked.

"Francesca," she said. "I get off here."

He walked with her till she stopped outside a typical archway leading into a cool courtyard of doors with brass plates and complicated names of companies and agencies.

"This is where I work, and I have to leave you now. But why don't we meet when I've finished, at eight o'clock?"

She was the one who was nervous now, nearly shaking with anxiety.

"All right," Juan said, wanting her to be calmer. "What's the time now?"

"Five, just after. In three hours time, right here, that door."

He watched her turn on her heels, walk across the courtyard and in through an entrance on the right.

He went on down the street bouncing on the balls of his feet a little, wanting to jump up, wanting to stop people and tell them about her, for now he had a friend. A girl friend.

On the hour, by the clock in a jeweller's shop opposite her office, he crossed the road and went through the arch into the courtyard to wait.

He realized it was a trap the moment two men stepped out of the shadows behind him. He turned, looking for a way out, and saw Francesca standing in a doorway.

Next to her was Brother Ignatius, smiling.

CHAPTER
— 7 —

The two men used silent persuasion rather than force.

They each took one of his wrists and led him into the building, past Francesca and Brother Ignatius, down a long corridor to an exit at the other end where two more men were waiting in a narrow street by a large car. One of them opened the door of the saloon and Juan was pushed into the back, not too gently, and one man got in on each side of him, the other two in front.

He did not struggle, did not attempt to resist them because of the expression in Francesca's eyes. She had played Judas, but had looked at him in such a way that he guessed she had no idea what she was doing and had been surprised by the appearance of the men herself. She had been used, had been duped into trapping him, but how that had come about would remain a mystery, not for ever perhaps, but certainly for now.

The car moved off down the road, curious people peering in at the four men in grey suits and the boy in the white T-shirt. The car was black and probably bore special number plates which those in the know would recognize as a vehicle of the Holy See.

They were taking him back to the monastery.

On the straight autoroute the driver slowed down unexpectedly and signalled another car on. It came swiftly from behind, black with the Vatican emblem flying. A cardinal's car and behind the white lace curtains the shape of Brother Ignatius.

He had played straight into Brother Ignatius's hands, had gone against Father Anthony's request to keep calm. Now, if they had the power, he would be locked up for good.

It was not Brother Ignatius he feared now, it was Father Anthony, the disappointment, the fact that he had let him down so, then failed to accomplish anything!

He saw the monastery up on the hill to the right, saw the Cardinal's car turn up the track leading to it. It was like going back to that school at the beginning of term. Exactly the same.

Inside the courtyard the Abbot was waiting.

"We have decided that you will remain in the vestments of your choosing having disgraced the habit of the Order; however, His Emminence has requested me to take you for confession, after which we will see if the Order has the heart to receive you back. We do not normally accept rebel spirits."

Juan felt like making a rude sign, or blowing a raspberry.

The Abbot led the way down the novices' cloister to the chapel, opened the door for him and let him pass into the cool familiar atmosphere of incense, candle smoke and devotion.

"May I see Father Anthony," Juan said as the Abbot made his way to the confessional.

"You may not."

"May I ask why not?"

The Abbot turned on his heels allowing his habit cord and rosary to fly out dramatically. He faced Juan with an expression of deep mortification.

"You have sinned against us, Brother Juan, and you have brought the monastery into disrepute. Be thankful that His Emminence, in his infinite wisdom and patience, has seen fit to grant you this chance to repent."

"I don't want to repent, Father," Juan said, "I wish to go, to leave the Order, to leave the monastery."

The Abbot made a sign of the cross.

"You do not want to confess?"

"No. It no longer means anything to me."

The Abbot took a deep breath, sighed at great length and studied him for a moment. He then closed his eyes and made the sign of the cross.

"I want to see Father Anthony," Juan said.

The Abbot moved away from him, strode up the three wide steps to the altar and from this more commanding position looked down on him. "Father Anthony, alas, is no longer with us. Moved by an evil spirit within him, he attempted to take his own life."

Juan could not believe it.

"He is recovering, we understand," the Abbot went on, "But as far as we are concerned he is in a state of excommunication."

"But where is he?"

"He was taken to the Hospital of Saint Cecilia."

"How . . . ?"

"Barbiturates, Brother Juan. Barbiturates. So shocked was he by your behaviour, so disappointed was he in his young pupil's thoughtless selfish action, that he apparently could not even turn to God for comfort."

There had to be more to it than that. Father Anthony would not attempt to take his life just because he, Juan, had escaped. The Abbot was over-dramatizing the situation as always. It was even possible that Father Anthony had just fallen ill.

*   *   *

Juan spent the next few weeks in a cell on the top floor of the monastery.

He was free to leave whenever he wished but had been requested to stay until official clearance had been received from the Vatican.

He was treated kindly, like a guest in a hotel.

He was not visited by anyone of authority, except a doctor who came to examine his physical health, and no one tried to bring him back to the faith.

He did not go to chapel, but on several occasions visited the cemetery and stood by Brother Martin's grave, half expecting a contact.

He met the Abbot by accident one day in a cloister, and requested the answers to a question.

"The girl Francesca, whose father died in Saint Cecilia's hospital and who led me back to you, who is she?"

"A devoted Christian, my son," had come the reply, "Who works in one of the many offices of the Holy See."

The Abbot had moved on, still smiling kindly, but making it clear that Juan's decision to leave the Order would never be forgiven.

So he had been right. They had probably told her he was mad.

As for Father Anthony, his action was a more closely guarded secret. On asking Brother Patrice how he was, he had been told "Better."

"What drove him to do such a thing?"

"Failure, Brother Juan, failure."

One day he was asked to present himself in Brother Ignatius's study after matins, and was made to wait a while before both the Brother Treasurer and his secretary monk came in.

"We have heard from His Emminence Cardinal Gregory

in Rome that we may permit you to take leave of the Order and the monastery providing you solemnly promise not to leave the country until you are eighteen and report your address to us once every month. Having reached the age of eighteen you are then legally no longer our responsibility and can do what you wish with your life."

Brother Ignatius opened a drawer and took out lire notes and postal money forms.

"In order to help you keep your promise, we will be retaining your passport here and giving you an allowance of 160,000 a month, approximately 40 dollars a week."

The monk pushed the money across the table.

"I can leave now?" Juan asked, surprised.

"Whenever you wish. The Abbot has asked me to tell you that should you have a change of mind and realize the error of your ways the monastery doors will always be open to you." It was said coldly as though it were not meant.

"Do you know the whereabouts of Father Anthony?" Juan asked.

"We do not, but if I may give you some advice, Brother Juan, *Mr* Juan, I would try to forget Father Anthony. What he did was not in your interest."

"What he did? What did he do?"

Brother Ignatius was going to vindicate himself and put everything in the right perspective, knowing that it would not be repeated in confession to the Abbot.

"Father Anthony lied, Mr Juan. Father Anthony lied to you, lied about you to us, lied about us to you. And all in order to be seen in a better light by His Emminence the Cardinal."

"In what way did he lie?"

"He invented a servant of the devil and called him Makar Boleslov in order to travel the world. He then fabricated the story that you were this man's son."

Had Brother Ignatius not seen the evidence of the documents? Probably not. Probably he had just been told of the circumstances by the Abbot.

"Is it known who my father is, then?" Juan asked.

"We suspect," Brother Ignatius said, pausing to overcome his own emotion, "We believe that it is Father Anthony himself."

Juan allowed his mouth to drop in astonishment.

"We have absolutely no proof, however," the Brother Treasurer went on. "Only he knows, only he could tell you if he were mentally stable. But alas, he is not, and can no longer be considered responsible for his actions."

He was out in the world again, this time for good, with no fears of priests policing the streets, with no fear of going hungry or of not having a bed.

In a year, when he was eighteen, the world would be his. Till then he would find work, after a holiday.

As he had been seen to the door by Brother Ignatius, he had asked about his family and had been told that they had been informed of the recent developments and that they would contact him if they so wished. He should not, however, expect them to do so. Unlike his grandfather and grandmother who had been devoted to the church, neither his aunt nor his uncle had shown much interest in Christian behaviour.

Juan walked all the way to Trasimeno and the familiar railway station. He took the first train to Rome where he knew he would feel most at home, and on arriving in the great city he walked towards the Gran Corso area which was most familiar to him and found a hostel on the way.

He was shown up to a large room on the first floor overlooking the noisy street, and once alone he leaned out of the window and stared down at the passersby, enjoying the sheer pleasure of being back in the land of the living.

Father Anthony, his father? His emotions were so mixed up about this. It was possible. Why had he been released, so simply, without the Abbot even saying goodbye? Why didn't he want to believe Brother Ignatius? Because he had enjoyed thinking of himself as someone special?

But then he was. Who else could communicate with the dead?

Two girls walked by, smart, slick on their delicate high heeled shoes, their calves working away, their breasts just hidden under the flimsiest of materials. It stirred something within him.

There was all that too. So much to be experienced, unlike Brother Martin, locked in his own skull in the depths of the damp earth.

He decided to go shopping, buy better trousers, a shirt or two, buy a map, see the city as a richer man.

He went into the same shop where he had bought the baggy trousers. He could afford better now. He looked through a stack of jeans and bought two pairs, beige and blue, and several T-shirts. In another shop he bought more comfortable sandals.

Now he would go back and change and then present himself at the hospital of Saint Cecilia to find out where Father Anthony had got to.

He bought a toothbrush, a razor, soap and toilet water. How extraordinary that all these things would be his to keep now.

It was as he climbed up the Spanish Steps back to the Hostel that he noticed the boy for the second time.

He was twelve, maybe more, with a dirty grey shirt, shorts and worn-out canvas shoes. The boy had been following him for quite a while. Was he working for the Vatican offices too?

At the top, making his way through the cars and taxis parked opposite the Hassler Hotel, the boy stepped out in front of him, blocked his way and thrust a card into his hand before running off, glancing to left and right, making sure he had not been seen.

Juan looked at what he had been given.

It was a piece of white cardboard the size of a visiting card. On one side was a very crudely drawn nine-pointed star within a circle, and on the other the words Villafossa, Binero, and the number three.

He slipped it into his pocket and walked quickly to his hostel. Once inside the safety of his room he looked at the card again. The sign was clearly to tell him who it was from. Someone who knew who he was, someone who knew everything. Father Anthony, alias Makar Boleslov? *Was* that possible?

He knew that Binero was Italian for "platform." Platform three. Platform three at a station called Villafossa? He would check with the receptionist.

Downstairs he was handed a guide to Rome, in the index he found Villafossa quickly enough, it was a suburb to the North.

When he reached Villafossa, and found Binero three there was no one around at all. It was mid-afternoon and not a soul was there, only the heat and the silence of a deserted railway station.

He walked up and down for a few minutes, looking for Father Anthony or perhaps a man with a beard, a bald man in a monk's habit, any man, anyone. The search was hardly difficult, he could see right up and down the platform, and across at the other two, even beyond at some of the houses of the suburb. He could see all the subway entrances.

He sat down on a bench and waited, losing confidence in his decision to have come so quickly. Then he saw her, timid in her familiar grey dress, standing across the track looking at him, about to go down the subway.

Francesca. He started down the steps, heard her footfall echoing in the passage below. They met halfway.

"Have you been followed?" she asked.

"I don't think so."

"Then come with me." She turned on her heels and led the way out of the station and along a deserted street, then up a road.

"Where are we going?" he asked.

"My house. There is someone there wanting to see you."

"Brother Ignatius?" he said, a little sharply.

"You must forgive me for that. I thought I was helping. That's the place, there."

The small house was up a gravel driveway overgrown with weeds. There had obviously been a magnificent mansion at the end but it had been cleared by bulldozers and there was only a building site now.

The small lodge, for that is what her house had been, had a slate roof and green shutters on faded yellow walls. There was a small garden with a dusty palm tree, dried up flower beds and an empty kennel. The whole place had the atmosphere of a once well-kept establishment gone to seed due to lack of money. The rusty gate hinges creaked as they stepped through, and he noticed now that every one of the shutters was closed.

She took him round the back to the kitchen door, and into a scullery with a stone floor and stone sink and a smell of earth. They went through into the kitchen itself, all white-tiled with a very old gas cooker and an equally old refrigerator, then into a living room so dark that she had to put on the light.

On a camp bed, lying under a blanket, was Father Anthony, hardly recognizable, so pale, so thin, so old had he become. How could anyone change in such a short time?

"He is here, Father," Francesca said, and left the room, closing the door.

Juan stepped forward to look down at Father Anthony. The priest smiled bravely and tried to lift a hand to shade his eyes from the light which was directly over him. But he was too weak.

"Could you . . ."

Juan switched off the offending bulb and waited till he became accustomed to the darkness. The room was cool, light coming through the slats of the shutters now, enough to see by.

"How have you been, Juan?" Father Anthony asked. The voice was a croak, there was a weariness in it that was unsettling.

"Well, thank you Father."

"You can no longer call me Father. I am a defrocked priest awaiting excommunication."

"I was told you were my real father," Juan said.

"And you believed it?"

"They told me you had lied to everyone."

"Why would I do that?"

"To hide the truth from me."

"The truth? What truth would I want to hide from you? What I revealed to you is surely worse than any truth. Which is why they tried to cover it up."

"Makar Boleslov is my father then?"

"Nothing I revealed was invention, Juan, nothing."

"Why did you contact me so secretly?"

"Because they are watching you. You will lead them to Boleslov sooner or later, so they are watching. Your release was not for your sake. It was for theirs. The war is still on. I am but one of the victims."

The effort to speak was too much for Father Anthony and he lifted his hand up for a moment and let it drop, as much as to say that he was giving up.

"Contact me Juan, that's all I beg you. Contact me when this stage is over, as you did with Brother Martin."

"Why did you try to take your life, Father?"

"They told me . . . they told me you were dead. They told me you had met with an accident and though I did not believe it was a simple accident, an innocent accident, I believed that you had been killed. I could not live without you Juan, because of my affection for you."

He closed his eyes and a peaceful expression came over his face.

Juan reached for Father Anthony's wrist, he felt his pulse. It was still beating, slowly, but still beating. He turned and saw Francesca standing there.

"How long has he been here?"

"Two weeks. He is getting weaker. He never quite recovered. It's best to let him sleep now. The doctor will be here later, he calls twice a day."

Juan did not want to leave, but Francesca was holding the door open. He followed her into the kitchen which was cloudy with steam.

"Are you hungry?" she asked.

"A little."

"I have made some pasta." She was nervous suddenly, wanted to be efficient. She opened the outside door to let the steam out, splashed the spaghetti into a colander, rinsed it, dropped it in another saucepan and mixed it all up with grated cheese.

She put it back on the stove and quickly laid the table

in the corner. She brought a bottle of wine out from a cupboard, a corkscrew from a drawer.

"Could you open that for me, or would you prefer something else?"

He opened the bottle. He had never opened a bottle in his life. He had seen others do it, his uncle, waiters in restaurants, waiters in films on television, but he had never opened a wine bottle in his life, that is how inexperienced he was.

He managed it without too much effort, without giving away his lack of education, and he poured the wine out in the glasses.

Though she was not trying to impress exactly, it was clear that she wanted things to be right to please him. He felt, for a moment, that they were really two children suddenly thrown into the grown up world playing at adulthood.

It was nearly fun.

Patiently he waited for her to start, then forked his spaghetti, twirled it, put it in his mouth.

It was really good, creamy as he had never had it before. The monastery spaghetti had been good too, but somehow not as good as this.

Thirsty, he drank his wine, rather fast, and she poured him out some more, but none for herself.

"It makes me feel dizzy," she said, "if I have more than one glass."

"Me too," he said.

The way she had poured it made him wonder if she was trying to get him drunk. Was she still working for the Papal agency? Surely not if Father Anthony had chosen to hide here.

"How did Father Anthony come to be here?" he asked.

"I heard what happened. I work for the Vatican press cutting office. One hears of most things there."

"Are you going to work there today?"

"No. I'm on holiday. A week I was owed. I have to go back Monday. Father Anthony insists so that things look normal. He was hoping that you would be found quickly. He would like you to stay, to look after him."

"I'll stay," Juan said, pleased that he could do something for the sick priest, "But what of my things at the hostel?"

"I'll take care of that. I've prepared a room for you. When we've finished lunch I'll take you up."

He ate some more, looking at her. She was so delicately beautiful, he had never seen anyone like her.

"How did you meet up with Father Anthony in the first place?" he asked.

"When he recovered sufficiently from his accident and was well enough to leave the hospital and return to the monastery, he was given a small sum of money and told *not* to return. It disgusted me so much that I went in search of him and found him in a small hostel in Trastevere. It was through him that I originally got my job. He taught me English for a year."

Juan knew so little about this man. He had been everywhere, knew everyone.

"What actually happened to him? What was the accident?"

"Didn't they tell you?"

"They told me nothing at all except that he tried to take his own life."

"When you left, when you disappeared, he informed the Cardinal personally that he had shown you certain documents relating to your parentage. He also told them that you were developing psychically more quickly than had been expected and that he understood perfectly why you had run away. This caused a furore in the Vatican circles, and he was then accused by certain monks and Cardinals of motivating you to escape. He was even accused of having a 'relationship' with you."

"A relationship?"

"They accused him of having a homosexual relationship with you, then accused him of being your real father. Then they told him you had met with an accident. He believed it. He had nothing else to live for."

Juan was silent for quite a while, aware that his head was buzzing, not only with the wine, but with all the things that were going on around him about which he was totally ignorant.

He had nearly been the cause of Father Anthony's death!

"Did you send the boy who found me and gave me that note?"

"Yes. I knew the day when you were to be released, I got three boys to watch out for you at the station and follow you."

"How much do you know about me?" Juan asked.

"Father Anthony has told me a great deal. He's talked of no one else since he's been here."

"And how much do you believe."

"Enough, or you wouldn't be here, would you?"

He smiled and sipped some more wine.

"Have you forgiven me?" she asked, fingering her empty glass nervously.

"For what?"

"For doing what I did to you, for giving you up to Brother Ignatius. I didn't know, you see. They told me Father Anthony was desperate to find you. My allegiance was to him. They were lying, of course, because already Father Anthony had taken his overdose."

There was so much he wanted to tell her, so much he could not. The wine was going to his head, he could feel the warmth, the glow, he wanted to laugh, to cry, he also wanted to hold her hand, hold her whole body close to his.

"Have you had enough?" she asked. "There is more."

"No . . . I've had plenty."

"Fruit? Grapes, oranges, or cheese? The apricots are ripe." She put the bowl of fruit on the table.

He sat back in his chair and peeled an orange, and she watched him. His hands got stickier and stickier and he wiped them on the clean napkin.

When he'd finished he got up to wash his hands, but she couldn't allow that. Guests washed their hands in the bathroom.

"I'll show you up to your room," she said.

She showed him the way up the stairs. "The bathroom is down here, my father put it in himself."

She left him, but he did not close the door. He just washed his hands and dried them on the clean crisp towel provided. As he walked out she said, "I'll show you the rest of the house," and threw open another door immediately to the right.

"This is my room. I used to sleep here with mother and father when we had a lodger. Otherwise I had your room. I couldn't get Father Anthony up the stairs, so I had to put him where he is." She closed the door.

They touched at the top of the stairs where it was narrow. She quite suddenly put her arms around him, her head on his shoulder and burst into tears.

"I'm so frightened," she said.

It was very natural the way he was able to hold her, hug her, rock her a little.

"What are you frightened of?"

"Everything. Death. It's been all around me for so long. Mother, a year ago, then father, now Father Anthony. I don't understand it. I don't understand what it's about. People who are with you one minute, not the next."

She laughed nervously and allowed herself to be hugged and he enveloped her slim body and it was a glorious feeling. He loved this girl, he really loved her, wanted to be with her for ever, wanted to do things for her for ever.

He pushed her away a little, just to look at her, then he kissed her. A first kiss, on the cheek, he had never kissed a girl before.

She turned her face so that their lips met and he felt her tongue press against his mouth. He opened his eyes, surprised, saw that hers were tight shut. He opened his mouth a little and felt her tongue in his mouth. It was a strange, delicate feeling. He had so much to learn.

She took his hand from behind her back and very gently, very gently, put it on her breast and pressed it there.

The sensation through the dress was quite extraordinary, he could feel the point of her nipple, could imagine her young breast underneath, like in Bronzino's or Piero di Cosimo's paintings.

Embarrassed he felt himself aroused, was worried lest she should become aware of him, down there.

But she quite suddenly broke away. "I must do the washing up," she said.

And left him standing there, bewildered.

For the next two days, over the week-end, Father Anthony hardly woke up at all.

A doctor came to visit him, not knowing who he was nor particularly caring and simply advised that he should be left to rest.

Each night they went separately to their respective rooms knowing full well that they would like to share each other, but also knowing that they could not with Father Anthony lying sick below.

Juan felt safer here than he had anywhere else in his life, aware that the responsibility he had been given of helping his tutor was helping him to overcome his constant fears.

On the Monday morning Francesca went off to work. Juan watched her go from behind the curtains of his bedroom to see if anyone followed her, but there was no one in evidence.

He moved silently about the house during the day, allowing Father Anthony as much sleep as possible. The priest seemed to be recovering, snored in fact, which somehow gave Juan confidence.

In the kitchen he washed up, but then, when letting the water out was aware that it gushed outside into a drain, neighbours therefore would know that someone else was in the house.

The postman came at about eleven, leaving a newspaper in the little tin box by the gate. Nothing else.

It was late in the afternoon, while he was sitting in the kitchen attempting to read *La Stampa,* an old copy he had found, that he heard the strange groan.

He rushed to Father Anthony's room and there saw the skeletal warning.

It had gone further than any other he had seen, even more than Francesca's father.

The skull was clean picked, the orbits black, the hands white with each bone delicately placed on the blanket, the backbone too, which he had never seen before. There were no tissues this time, it was the purest image of death he had seen.

The apparition beckoned and opened its mouth. "Juan . . ." The voice was a gasp. "Juan . . . come sit down here by me and listen . . . listen very closely . . ."

Juan sat down. Death was talking to him, wanting to hold his hand.

"I am going to die very shortly . . . as you can see . . . and you have much to learn . . . much . . ."

Juan looked away for a moment, and when he looked back he saw that life was seeping back into the priest's shape. There was a recognizable face with pale skin, eyes staring ahead, hands with the fingers and knuckles and nails.

"You are being watched, not right now perhaps, but you will constantly be watched because you will lead them to Boleslov, and they want to be rid of him. You are the only person who can lead them to him, because he must be seeking you."

Father Anthony took a deep breath and somehow found the strength to pull himself up a little, then breathing very heavily, a rattling coming from his ribs, he said, "Contact me however hard it is, for I may find the answers to so many things. Brother Martin was a simple man and . . ."

He did not finish the sentence but closed his eyes.

Juan, sitting on the bed holding the priest's hand took a deep breath and forced himself to remain exactly where he was and watch.

The face quite suddenly took on a look of incredible peace, the eyes closed, the muscles relaxed, a very slight smile danced on the lips. He waited for the deterioration, waited for the tissues to melt away, for the veins to show through, for the awful eyes to turn yellow and sink back into the orbits, but nothing happened. The face remained serene, white like marble, and when he touched it the coldness of the skin told him that Father Anthony was dead.

He bent over immediately and pressed his forehead against the dead brow.

It took but a few seconds, the hiss, but unlike Brother

Martin's it did not come from a great distance but was there, right there in the skull and then seemed to recede very slowly.

"Father Anthony?" Juan said out loud.

The hiss grew fainter.

"Father Anthony?"

There was nothing now. Nothing at all. So Juan stood up, pulled the blanket up and over Father Anthony's head, and left the room. Never had he felt such a terrible sense of loss as now. By running away he had caused his only friend's death.

CHAPTER
— 8 —

Francesca came home at half past seven. Juan looked out for her from an upstairs window, saw the childlike figure coming along the road, and he rushed downstairs and waited in the kitchen for her to open the door.

When she came in he dared kiss her briefly.

"How is Father Anthony?"

He could not say it. He could not bring himself to say it, so she understood, patted his hand and went to the living room, did not go right in but just opened the door a little to look at the body covered by the blanket.

"It was inevitable," she said, "It was what he wanted." She closed the door. "Did he talk to you much?" she asked, returning to the kitchen.

"Hardly at all. He did not seem to have the energy."

"He had so much to say to you. He talked about you as though you were a . . . well as though you were a saint."

Juan felt the remark embarrassing. "I'm not that, I can assure you."

And she smiled, put out her hand affectionately and squeezed his arm gently.

"What do we do now?" Juan asked.

"I will call on the doctor and funeral directors and have him buried in the local cemetery."

"Won't there be complications?"

"None that can't be overcome. I will tell the authorities he was an uncle, my mother's brother. He was as good as an uncle to me. It's the least I can do."

Francesca went to fetch the doctor immediately and returned with him shortly.

He examined Father Anthony rapidly, the eyes, the pulse, listened to the heart with his stethoscope, crossed the dead man's hands over his chest and replaced the blanket over his face.

She had just been through the rituals of a death with her father, knew what had to be done, the routine. She saw the doctor to the door while Juan stayed in the room with the corpse wondering what he would do next.

He had no plans but knew that he would have to make contact again before the funeral, during the night when Francesca was asleep, that was the time to do it.

Had Father Anthony taken his own life for this purpose he wondered, had he speeded his life's end so that he could communicate with him from the next world? Suicide seemed such a senseless and uncharacteristic thing to do. Father Anthony had never been one for self pity, for lack of confidence.

Was it possible that Father Anthony had been murdered? He would find out. Tonight he would find out. Tonight he would be in contact with Father Anthony and ask him to answer what he had been unable to answer in life.

But the night did not turn out at all as he had planned.

They ate a pizza she had spent Sunday preparing, and drank a little more wine than usual to push away the inevitable sadness.

Juan decided that he would wait till dawn perhaps, then

go down to the living room and make the contact. In the dead of night he would have to put on a light, and that could disturb Francesca if she were a light sleeper for she always left the door wide open.

After he helped her wash up and put away the two plates, the two glasses, the knives and forks, she hung up her apron as usual, pulled him to her and kissed him on the mouth.

Surprised, he did not react very romantically, so she held on to his hand and led him up the stairs.

A light in her room was already on, the small table lamp next to the bed with the dark green shade over it. The bed itself, with clean white sheets under a soft counterpane, was turned down. To his astonishment she closed the door and immediately started to unbutton her dress.

She moved to one side of the bed as she slipped the dress off and stepped out of her sandals. She then turned to face him in her small tight bra and pants and got into bed, staring at him all the while with her wide grey-blue eyes, a sensuous smile playing on her lips. He was unable to move, aware that his heart was beating incredibly fast.

Then she switched off the light. In the dark he kicked off his shoes, unzipped his jeans, peeled off his shirt and in his briefs climbed into the soft warm bed next to her.

He did not have time to think what he should do, he was aware of his excitement, of his erectness, and he was strangely embarrassed by it, not wanting her to feel him in this condition. He would rather have been limp, felt it would be more polite, but she threaded one hand under his head, round his shoulders, under his arm, and pulled him towards her, and with her other hand found him tight there within his briefs.

Her fingers were cold around him. He could feel each one along his length, and he could feel how burning hot he was. Her lips found his mouth, they kissed, they embraced, she was so eager, so warm. She pressed herself against him and he felt the touch of her covered breasts pressing flat against his chest, felt their flexibility, their softness and he moved his hand over them, over their firmness, moved his hand down, on the flat of her stomach, the tips of his fingers finding their way under the elastic and touching the brittle yet soft hair.

She moved away for a moment, sat up, pulled her knees up, and when she came back to him she was completely naked.

She helped him off with his briefs, held him very tightly.

He felt the hair between her legs, the soft warm crease, the wetness, and she started caressing him now so that the feeling was unbearable.

He moved over her, pushed her gently onto her back, lay on top of her and, as though he had done this before a hundred times, as though he were an expert lover, he guided himself into her, and gasped at the warmth and ecstacy of it all. How could priests and monks refuse themselves this natural joy? How mad was the church to forbid the messengers of their faith to taste God's most precious gift?

The unexpected pleasure was her pleasure, her little whimperings, her breathing, her sudden and surprisingly vicious movements as he did something to her which seemed beautifully unbearable. Then his excitement rose to fever pitch and, frightened of being selfish, he tried to hold back, but could not.

He groaned with pleasure and moaned with regret and she comforted him with words he did not understand, caressing his forehead as though he were in need of comfort, kissing him as though he were a child. Was this part of woman's pleasure, to nurse the unbearably satisfied?

Wrapped in her arms, her limbs, not leaving her body but holding her more tightly than before, he felt himself slip into a delirious oblivion and only when she woke him up the next morning and he had taken a sip of the milky brown coffee she had made him did he realize with an agony of guilt that he had totally forgotten Father Anthony.

The familiar hauntings began shortly after the funeral. They were in his conscience, in his mind as they had been before, they affected no one but him, but they were real.

When both his grandparents and Magdalena had died he had seen them again as ghosts, hideous skeletal images appearing suddenly where he least expected them. At the foot of his bed, on a street corner, sitting next to him in a car, they had caused him to scream in the night, sometimes in broad daylight, which had prompted his aunt and uncle to seek the advice of a psychiatrist.

The doctor's wife drove Francesca to the local cemetery. He watched the departing hearse and the little Fiat following behind it from the upstairs window.

When he turned round the apparition was standing in the doorway, the skull picked clean, the white boned hands beckoning.

"I don't know how, but I *will* contact you. I promise," he said out loud shutting his eyes.

He counted up to ten, slowly, willing the apparition to go away, to leave him alone, and when he opened his eyes it had indeed gone.

Juan debated with himself the whole day whether he should tell Francesca or not. He had two allegiances now. One was to Father Anthony and the search for Makar Boleslov, to make that contact somehow as though it were his life's work, as though he had been born for that purpose, the other was now to Francesca.

Could the two be fused? Could Francesca help him?

He lay awake that night next to her not knowing how

much he should tell her, how much she would believe if he told her.

When she returned from the funeral they had gone to bed again, at five in the afternoon, unable to resist each other, longing to repeat the pleasures of the night before. But what future could he promise her, what was he offering other than necromantic madness? It was eleven, a hot night, he got up to go to the bathroom.

"Can't you sleep either Juan?" she asked in the dark.

"No . . ."

"Would you like a lemonade? I will make some lemonade."

He would tell her, he would tell her down in the kitchen. Though he had decided it would be wiser to talk about it during the day when things would seem less lugubrious, he also knew that this would be a good moment. They were so close now.

He slipped on his jeans and joined her in the kitchen. He watched her cut two lemons, squeeze them hard on the sharp metal point of the squeezer, pour the pure juice in two long glasses, add water, sugar, ice and stir them both. She handed him the cool glass. It was delicious.

"What are we going to do now?" he started.

"Go back to bed?"

"I didn't mean right now, I meant tomorrow, the day after, the week after . . . what are we going to do with the future?"

"I have to work. We have to have money."

"I have to work too."

"To buy your ticket for America?"

"I hadn't thought of leaving just yet."

"You can stay here," she said.

He had taken that for granted. "Francesca," he said more earnestly, "I have something to do, something I must do alone, something with which you cannot help me and about which I cannot speak until I have done it."

"You have your life Juan. You do not belong to me, you do not owe me any explanations."

"In my mind I do," he said, and she smiled, understanding what he meant.

"I have this . . . thing to do . . . at night. I can only do it at night, a vigil, if you like, connected with Father Anthony. A promise I have to keep. And once I have fulfilled this promise I will be free to decide what I can do, what I want to do. I know that I would like to take you away from here, somehow."

They went back to bed refreshed by the drink, cooler, and fell asleep in each other's arms.

The next day he kissed her by the kitchen door as she left for work and told her that he might not be there when she got back. He would be home later, maybe in the early hours of the morning.

As soon as she had gone and he had made sure that there were no neighbours taking particular interest in the activities of the house, he slipped out into the garden to the small potting shed next to the old dog kennel.

As he had hoped, he found exactly what he needed, a spade, a small axe and a rusty screwdriver which he could sharpen.

Back in the house he searched for something to wrap up the implements, discovered a pile of old newspapers underneath the stairs and made a parcel which hid the shape of the spade. In a drawer he unexpectedly found a pencil torch which worked. It would be ideal, he pocketed it. He had the whole day to wait now, a whole day to himself, a whole day to think through his life and its meaning, if it had ever had any.

Out of all the confusion of the last month what could he

salvage that he believed in, what did he really think was the truth?

Makar Boleslov was true. Father Anthony had been appointed Boleslov's investigator. Eventually he had found Boleslov's son.

Where he had failed Father Anthony was in not understanding the pressure he must have been under from the Cardinals, indeed not even being aware of it. Was that his fault?

Father Anthony had to take some of the blame for having been secretive for so long. It must have been the realization that he had made a terrible mistake in showing him the documents, the ultimate mistake, sealing his fate as far as the others were concerned, signing his death warrant, that had made him take his life. They had lied to him, told him he had had an accident, and he couldn't live with that.

Juan hoped that during the contact he would be able to apologize, would be able to convey the terrible regret, would be forgiven. For was that not what he wanted now, forgiveness?

He missed the confessional.

Hadn't it made life easy?

You sinned, you confessed, you were absolved.

Penalty—a few prayers.

Faith was indeed wonderful, a miracle in fact.

At six he left the house, made sure he was not being followed, and made his way to the local cemetery.

It was some distance away, a good three miles, but he enjoyed the walk for it took him to the edge of the suburbs and closer to the real countryside.

He had timed it so that he would be among the evening visitors to the cemetery, lost in the small crowd that filtered in and out of the gate.

He found Father Anthony's unmarked grave easily enough, recognized the wreath of flowers Francesca had bought. He did not stay near it for long, but walked around looking for a suitable hiding place.

In the shadows of several cypress trees there was a mausoleum of brown-red marble with a wrought iron gate which had no lock. He stood before it, reading the inscription.

When he was sure he was alone, that no one could see him, he stepped through the gate, into the mausoleum to hide behind the pillars and crouched down to await nightfall.

He had no watch but quickly enough learnt the time from the different bells that sounded in the clock towers of the surrounding district.

He waited till eleven, then could wait no longer.

He moved out of his hiding place and walked swiftly to Father Anthony's grave. He was tense, pent up with emotion as though he were going to meet someone at a rendezvous.

Unlike his previous nocturnal excavation, there was no moonlight, but his eyes were sufficiently accustomed to the dark for him to see what he was doing.

He moved the soft earth to one side easily enough, then he dug his spade in. He pushed the clods away, occasionally hit a large stone, scattered the earth, not caring how much of a mess he made. He had no idea, of course, how deep the grave would be, but he suspected it would be no deeper than three feet. He worked hard, ceaselessly, and eventually his spade struck the top of the coffin.

It sounded hollow, as though the box were empty.

He worked faster, clearing the earth, shining the little torch down to see how much more he had to do.

It was a different shaped coffin to Brother Martin's, the lid was secured by screws in the side. He had to move quite a lot more earth to get at them, but he did it, without a break, thankful that he could now allow himself a short period of rest.

Feeling the grooves of the screws with his finger tips he fitted the screwdriver in and turned. It was not easy as he had to work at an angle, but eventually he got them all out and was able to prize the lid open.

The odour was fearful.

An acrid smell of putrescence forced him to hold his nose and breathe through his mouth. When he touched the shroud he realized it was sticky with a body substance that had oozed out.

He put one foot on either side of the coffin rim and reached down to pull up the body.

It was wrapped, like a mummy, and was very heavy.

He nearly lost his balance when the legs buckled and he heard a sickening wrench as he swung the corpse to lay it on the grass.

He would not undo the shroud, he would not look, he would feel for the forehead and keep his distance from the rest of the body.

As before he knelt at the head, bent forward holding his breath, held the top of the skull between his hands and pressed his brow against it.

He closed his eyes and it came, the sound, the hiss, very loud, so loud that he instinctively put his hands to his ears only to realize that of course the noise was within his head, within both their heads, a hollow sound as though it were whirring round the cavities of a massive skull or the endless corridors of a marble maze.

"Father Anthony?"

"Yes... yes I am here..." It was a weary voice, disillusioned, frail, pleading.

"Can I help you?"

CATACOMB   119

The answer took a long time to form itself into coherent words. It was there, could be sensed but was not at first intelligible.

After a number of strangled attempts it came out, distinctly.

"*Help?*"

"Can I help you?"

"*Yes . . . help . . .*"

"How can I help you Father? How can I help you and others?"

"*Yourself . . . help yourself . . .*"

"Help myself? Helping myself will help you?"

"*Progress . . . progress . . . your father . . .*"

"Who is my father . . . where is my father?"

"*With you . . . he is with you . . .*"

"Where?"

There was no answer.

"Can I always contact you like this?"

"*Yes . . .*"

"Will you go away like you did last time?"

"*Yes . . .*"

"Is our time limited then?"

"*Energy is limited. Energy . . .*"

"Your energy or my energy?"

"*My energy . . .*"

"Can you move from where you are?"

"*No . . .*"

"Will you move when I release you . . . if I can release you?"

"*Oh . . . yes . . .*"

"Will you return?"

There was no answer.

"Will you return, is there reincarnation?"

There was a long pause. The contact had not been lost,

the line was still open, Juan could feel this, then quite suddenly the voice came through much clearer with renewed energy.

"We return if we wish, but we forget everything on returning. The process of learning to desire is all the system needs. The process of learning to desire. Human desire is energy. Fulfilment of desire in all its facets is energy and that is all the system expects of you."

"Desire?" Juan repeated, "Any desire?"

"Anything . . . anything . . . anything."

"What of desire to be pious?"

"That is a desire to escape, it is self deception, but it is still a desire . . ."

"What is evil then, Father?"

"Repression of any sort is evil, real evil, those who try to stop others doing what they desire is evil, it is against basic nature."

"Can we choose when we die, was what you did evil?"

"Life is an accident . . . and so is death . . . All deaths are accidental . . . things happen because they are out of control. The human lives longer than the animal because he has more control. That is all. Illness is accidental, you can prevent illness."

"Are you in limbo, a kind of limbo?"

"I am in my head Juan. I am in my head . . ."

"Are there millions of dead like that then . . . ?"

"All the dead, all the buried, countless millions."

"Are they desperate?"

"Most are unaware. They are without desire."

"What matters in life Father?"

"Nothing matters Juan. We are so unimportant. There is no real progress to be made, there is no ambition that is not a fantasy, for we cannot become God because God is a system which does not listen, which does not hear."

"What of prayer Father. You believed so much in prayer."

"Prayer is verbal desire, it means nothing in itself unless it is fulfilled, then it produces energy."

"Is something expected of us? Is something expected of me? Why was I chosen to be able to communicate with . . . you?"

"We expect you to help us by destroying us, but you were not chosen. You are an accident desired by your father, who sought and found the answer to the mystery of death."

"Destroy you? I don't understand."

"We are all alike in death, all condemned by the unknown to wait our own slow physical deterioration till nothing is left. You must therefore destroy."

"I still don't understand."

"Burn, Juan. Burn us. Fire is total extinction, our minds cannot be released till we no longer exist. The pattern you see. The incredible pattern we cannot understand demands it. Your father understands. Has learnt. Ashes to ashes is immediate, dust to dust can take centuries of madness with no one to tell . . ."

"Then all we have been taught is wrong?"

"All we have been taught is . . . counter productive . . ."

It was a phrase they had laughed at, a phrase from a financial article in an American magazine that Father Anthony had received from a friend.

"The desire to kill, what of that?"

"Why are there wars, Juan?"

"The desire to self indulge?"

"Desire is self indulgence. Its fulfilment is energy. The system, the pattern thrives on that energy."

"What is the system?"

"Look up at the sky now and you will understand how little you can ever understand."

Juan looked up automatically, stared at the vast sky above, the stars, the milky way, the beyond he could not see because it was so endless, and when he put his head back against Father Anthony's he knew the contact had gone.

"Father Anthony?" he said. "Father Anthony, I'll be back. I promise. I cannot come every night . . . I cannot come and do this . . . every night . . . but I will come back and I will arrange for your cremation . . . somehow I will do that but I must have time . . . I must have more time . . ."

He kneeled back, straightened up, still holding the dead head in his hands.

He was gaining knowledge, gaining incredible knowledge which could never be taken from him.

He stood up and looked at the stars again, at the infinite universe which was only part of the system, the pattern. Why had no one broken through the death barrier before? Or had they and decided not to tell?

Would he want to tell? If he wanted to tell, then he would. Didn't his desirous love of Francesca prove some of what he had learnt to be right, the very joy of it? And yet fulfilment of desire on earth could get you into trouble, so many desires were against the law. It was not that easy, the system's wishes.

Curious now to see Father Anthony's face, Juan bent down and removed the shroud back from the head. He had stopped himself from uncovering him before because he felt it undignified, ghoulish, but now he desired it, so did it, and he stared down at the tight skinned face with matted hair with its eyes closed, and its thin lips. He thought he saw something small and white wriggle out of the nose, and he threw the shroud across the face again and kicked the body back into the coffin.

It was no longer Father Anthony, or anything to do with the voice he had heard, it was just the foul evidence of death.

He dropped the lid back on, aware that the inside was alive with maggots. He was suddenly terrified at the idea of maggots crawling all over him, and he started kicking the earth back in the hole, shovelling it in violently, imagining worms crawling up his trouser legs.

He would never do this again.

Never.

He felt something tickling the back of his neck and he whipped round to flick it off. As he did so he saw a movement in among the trees by the cemetery gates. A faint movement, a grey shape which could have been a man. He remained quite still. Was someone watching him, or was it a ghost?

Whatever it was, he wanted to leave. He had had enough, his imagination could no longer be separated from reality, he could not recognize which was which. He left the spade stuck in the grave, walked quickly away, then started running.

He ran.

It could have been five miles, it could have been seven, he had no idea and he did not care.

He ran, then he walked in the night, taking wrong turnings, getting lost, but not caring.

He had been in contact with the dead, he had talked again to Father Anthony. However revolting the experience, he had done it and now was more knowledgeable about the after life than anyone else on earth.

You remained in your skull. You were your own brain until it deteriorated and rotted away. Fire was the release after which there was still another mystery. What of reincarnation then?

He would have to talk to Father Anthony again, only through him would that mystery be revealed.

And what of Boleslov? Would this man ever show up? *"He is with you . . ."* Father Anthony had said, but where? Had he been the shadow, watching?

A car passed him. It passed him so slowly that it suggested the driver was thinking of picking him up. He thought little of it until the same car appeared again later down a side street, parked with at least two people in it. He started running again, realizing now where he was. He had missed the road he knew, but was not far from home. In his anxiety to get away from the cemetery fast he had in fact apparently circled it. He was near home.

Had Francesca's little house become his home then? He turned the final corner past the station, up the familiar gravel road and went through the gate and round the back to the kitchen.

He closed the door, bolted it, switched on the light and looked at his clothes, smelt his hands. He had got used to the odour, but now, indoors, it was strong and revolting. He took everything off and washed himself as quietly as he could. Stripped naked he sponged himself down as he had so often in his cell at the monastery.

The water was cold, refreshing, he put all his clothes in the sink and let the tap run on them, then he turned and saw her standing in the doorway watching him.

Her eyes asked where he had been, but she said nothing. He had told her he had something special to do, he had also implied that when it was done a problem would be resolved. Well it was not. How could he explain that?

She disappeared for a moment then returned with a large towel and an old dressing gown. He dried himself, put the dressing gown on. He sat down at the table, accepted the cup of coffee she made, a piece of bread, cheese. He was hungry. He had not realized how hungry he was. His whole mind had been concentrated on that voice.

She sat down opposite him, neat, clean, smelling of cologne in a near transparent nightdress, her hands and fingers so beautiful, the line of her lips so perfect.

He wanted to kiss her. So he did. He stood up, leaned right across the table and gently kissed her lips, leaving a crumb on them which she delicately picked off with her tongue.

"Can you talk about it?" she asked, breaking the silence.

"I don't know . . ."

"Will you be here when I get back from work tomorrow?"

"Yes."

She asked nothing more but just watched him eat, watched him stir his coffee and drink it.

They went upstairs holding hands. He lay down in the comfort of the large bed, there was a smell in the room which was partly her, partly someone he had never known. Her father, her mother?

God, could he contact her father? Should he do so, should he release him from the agony of the skull? He closed his eyes. A nightmarish hood of blackness overwhelmed him, a drowsiness which he fought, fearing it, fearing it like the shroud, like the look on Father Anthony's face when he had dared look at it.

He slept fitfully throughout the next day. At some time he got up feeling hungry, fed himself more bread, more cheese, returned upstairs and went to sleep again. Later he made himself some coffee and sat in the room where Father Anthony had died.

There was nothing of him in the room, only the smell of surgical spirit and polish. It had all been cleaned up and put back the way Francesca's mother would have liked it.

Shortly after eight Francesca came home, tired after the

train ride in the heat. He had thought of preparing her something, but had not known what.

"They asked me about you today."

"Who?"

"Certain people at the office."

"What did they ask?"

"Whether you still lived here."

"*Still?* So they know I've been here a few days?"

"I think they know everything."

"Everything?"

"They know where you were last night. What you did."

He couldn't believe it. "What did I do?"

She hesitated, was embarrassed a little by what she was going to say as though it might not be true and he would think the fantasy ridiculous. "They said that you went to the cemetery and dug up Father Anthony's body . . . and talked to it."

So he *had* been watched.

"Is that what you did?" she asked.

"Yes."

"Why?"

"I can talk to the dead," he said simply, "I can communicate with the dead."

She looked at him but he was unable to guess what she was thinking.

"Are you worried that I'm mad?" he asked.

"Before you came here Father Anthony asked me to look after you unquestioningly," Francesca said. "He told me you were an exceptional boy with an exceptional gift."

"There is a sort of life after death," he said, "But it is a void. Father Anthony is now in limbo, his voice comes from an inner space in his head."

"How do you hear his voice?"

"I put my forehead against his, the communication seems to come through that contact."

"How did you know what to do? Who taught you?"

"It just happened by accident, at the monastery when a brother died." He sensed he could talk naturally to her about it all now, and it was a great relief. So he told everything. About his life at the monastery, about his virtual imprisonment, about the file, the documents, it all came out, flowed out. He told her about his mother, about Boleslov. Even admitted that he sometimes felt that his father was the devil, but that that was ridiculous since the devil did not exist, nor in fact did God.

"It explains a great deal," Francesca said after a while, getting up to peel some vegetables for the evening meal.

"What does it explain?"

"If life after death is a void, if there is no God, no Jesus Christ, no Virgin Mary as we understand them, then it totally negates religion, Christian religion and others."

"So what does it explain?"

"It explains why you are being watched day and night, and why you will go on being watched until you come up with something on which they have to act."

"Such as?"

"A pronouncement. Or your father making an appearance. Obviously you have inherited these powers from him."

"You regard them as powers?"

"I regard them as powers, yes. Powers to upset a thousand years of beliefs. And if you can speak to the dead, Juan, imagine what you can find out about the past!"

"I can't imagine," Juan said, truthfully.

"Did Father Anthony say nothing to you of what you should do, of what might be expected of you?"

"What we do with our lives is not important."

"You don't think that if you contacted him again he could advise you what to do?"

"How can I contact him again? I couldn't disinter . . ." Everything seemed so unreal now with her standing by the sink peeling potatoes, talking to him about a conversation he had had with a dead man.

"Did they watch me all night then?" he asked.

"Yes."

"Am I being watched now?"

"Yes. They're outside."

"Why did they tell you?"

"They still think I am working for them, Juan. They believe that I am working for them when I am not. I am working for you and for Father Anthony and, maybe, for my father."

He stood up suddenly feeling oppressed as though his head would burst. "How can I get rid of them?"

"Why not use them?"

"How do you mean?"

"You want to talk to Father Anthony again don't you, to others? I can tell them that you have told me that Father Anthony has a message for them."

"What good will come of that?"

"Did you enjoy digging up the grave?"

"No."

"They would do all that for you, they would disinter Father Anthony and clean him up and you could communicate with him under more scientific circumstances."

He suspected that the idea was not hers, that she had been asked to suggest it to him. The point was that it was a good idea if they were willing to help him. He didn't want to go through another night of digging, suffer further fears and nightmares of maggots and worms.

"Could they get some recording equipment so that what I hear could be taped . . . me repeating it?"

"I can ask. There is no harm in asking."

She was still working for them, he sensed it. She was beautiful and delicate and pretended vulnerability, but she was also very intelligent. Francesca was on the agency staff, he was sure of it.

The idea that she had so easily won him over, so easily made him believe that she loved him, suddenly made her more desirable, but in a different way. When he had made love to her the first time he had checked a need to be violent. Well, desire should not be checked, according to Father Anthony, desire and its fulfillment was what made the world go round. So he would use the little Francesca, he would take her now for what she was. He would use her, and he would use them!

CHAPTER
— 9 —

When he awoke the next morning he was surprised to find himself in the middle of the bed cosseted between two pillows. Francesca was sitting close to him holding a breakfast tray of toasted bread and milky coffee.

"What time is it?" he asked.

"Eleven. You were very tired."

"What about your work?" he asked, concerned that she would be late.

"I rang them up, told them of our conversation last night. I am to ring them again later."

Had she duped Father Anthony as well, made *him* believe she was a friend. He reached out for her. He kissed her lightly, because of the breakfast tray which forbad anything more, and she pushed him away gently.

"Eat, you must regain your strength."

"I must? I've been resting all day yesterday and had a good night's sleep."

"No, a good night you didn't have. You were haunted in your dreams, I could tell by the way you groaned."

After a mouthful or two, staring at her, looking at her beautiful face, her body, understanding now why he had been allowed to possess it so easily, but feeling the excitement rising again in his nakedness under the sheet, he said, "Is anyone watching the house?"

She nodded.

"In a car?"

"No. Just a man, near the building site pretending to be a workman. But I know him."

He drank his coffee, picked up the tray, dropped it with a clatter on the floor and turned to her.

"What *are* you doing?" she asked.

He pulled her to him.

"No . . . Juan . . ."

He kissed her, kissed her neck, under her ears, under the ear lobes, he undid her neat bun and let her hair flow down her back. She was wearing a skirt and a blouse, with difficulty he undid the little buttons down the back, an impossible garment to remove without a great deal of struggle. He found the zip of her skirt, undid that.

"No . . . Juan . . . I have the washing up to do . . ."

He turned her round forcefully so that she had to lie on the bed, she was not strong, not strong at all. She suddenly relaxed to let him have his way.

Another game, another pretence. He lifted her skirt, looked at the length of her silky legs, the tight white underpants. He pulled them down. Her eyes were closed, she was waiting, passively. He pulled the pants down and looked at the soft curly black hair. He bent down and kissed the flat of her stomach, her hand immediately moved to the back of his head.

He was solid now and he moved on top of her, and into her and squeezed her, kneading her breasts, wanting to be the male animal who could hurt. He stopped to remove her blouse. She pretended not to help but managed to put her arms out so that it was easier for him. He let it drop to the floor. Now there was only her bra which he unclipped.

She was totally naked now, her eyes still closed, biting her lower lip in a way of conveying pleasurable sin. He kissed her, bit her, moved aggressively inside her, the fever caught him and the rougher he was the more aroused she became. She moaned, wriggled, scratched his back in the ecstacy she was feeling. Then he felt the climax coming, did not care whether she was with him or not, thrust more urgently, more quickly, wanting the suspense of delicious agony to be over.

And suddenly it was. A draining of his very being, the million seeds escaping from him. He remained taut for a few seconds, then gave in, collapsed on her, covering her.

He wondered whether she had been sensible and taken precautions or whether she would have his child. And somehow he didn't care. He would quite like the idea of her having a child, his child, but it was not important.

She kissed him gently on the forehead and told him to rest, then got up and left the room. He heard her in the bathroom, watched her as she came back in with a towel which she threw over him. No shyness anymore, she wandered around nude, opened a drawer, took out another pair of tiny pants, slipped them on. Her body was so slim. Her breasts, in no way large, were so exciting.

"I love you," he said, putting his arms behind his head and stretching out. "Will you marry me?"

"When you're twenty one," she said.

"That's years away."

"Then it gives me time to think about it."

"What if you have a child?"

"I am not a nun, my sweet little monk. In this great modern world we have ways of arresting the population. These," she said, and threw him a small plastic envelope with rows of yellow pills.

She left the room to go downstairs and he got up and

looked out of the window. To the left was the building site and sitting in the shadows of an unfinished wall was a man, smoking, looking innocent.

Juan went to the bathroom and had a cold shower. He gasped at the instant shock, but it felt good afterwards. To think he had always washed with cold water, even in the middle of winter.

He heard a loud knock on the front door and, drying himself, went to the bedroom to look out of the window again.

A black car had drawn up outside the house, a man in a grey suit was waiting in the garden and the builder-spy was talking to the chauffeur.

He heard Francesca open up and say something rapidly in Italian. The door closed, the man in the grey suit got into the car, the builder-spy as well, and all drove off.

"It's from the Cardinal's office," Francesca shouted, coming up the stairs.

She ran into the room reading a note she had taken out of a long white envelope.

"He is proposing a meeting at four o'clock this afternoon."

"The Cardinal himself, Cardinal Gregory?"

"Yes, Cardinal Gregory. They'll send a car."

"Is there any option to refuse?"

"I wouldn't have thought so. They might stop your monthly allowance." It was said with a smile, light heartedly, and it gave her away.

He had never told her about the financial arrangements Brother Ignatius had made. She had clearly been told everything, she was their spy.

Before the appointed hour she took him to buy some presentable clothes. She bought him a dark blue two piece he didn't like, a white shirt with a blue tie he didn't like and blue socks and black shoes which were very uncomfortable.

To make up for it, however, she bought him an unexpected present. He stopped to look into a souvenir shop window.

"You want a souvenir of Rome?" she asked.

"I'd like that lighter."

"But you don't smoke."

"I know, but I've always wanted a lighter. My uncle wouldn't give me one, he said they were dangerous. Now they have those thin flat ones with gas. Look at the red one!"

"It's an advertisement for an American cigarette."

"I like the colour."

"Then I'll buy it for you."

And she did.

She had bought everything for him and though at first he had offered to make some contribution she waved his money aside in such a way that it was clear she would get it back on some expense sheet or other.

At four o'clock he put his head in the lion's mouth.

The meeting took place in one of the Vatican buildings and he was received like a visiting diplomat and made a fuss of by the Cardinal's officers. The greetings were cordial and as informal as they could be with the Cardinal himself, a Bishop and two Deacons present. He had not realized that there were such luxurious drawing rooms within the Vatican with velvet seats, a fireplace, paintings of great value on the walls and priceless antique furniture everywhere he looked.

They had tea to drink and little cakes and biscuits offered by a servant in a white jacket, before anything was said officially.

Francesca was shy and sat, like a schoolgirl again, on the edge of her armchair, both hands in her lap, as good as gold.

Cardinal Gregory, in his red robes, sat on a more throne-like chair, higher than the Bishop and the Deacons, enabling him to look down at everyone regally.

Juan had to make an effort not to feel small, and tried to think of what he had done, who he might be, the powers he had.

"Brother Juan," the Bishop said, obviously speaking on behalf of the Cardinal, coming straight to the point, "You have suffered a number of unpleasant experiences since leaving the walls of the monastery, you have also suffered the loss of Father Anthony whom we all know was your beloved tutor. Some of us believe that this may have affected your reasoning, others, considering your background about which you of course know, are ready to give you the benefit of the doubt. Whatever else, you have committed two offences punishable by law, that of disinterring first Brother Martin at the Monastery of Trasimeno, and then Father Anthony in the cemetery of Villafossa, which puts us in a position of being able to withdraw the privileges accorded to you. Are we making ourselves clear?"

Juan nodded, tried to look at the Cardinal, but the old man was examining him so closely that he had to look away and down at his feet.

"Now," the Bishop continued, "We understand that you claim to have been in contact with Brother Martin since he died, using supernatural means. Is that correct?"

"Yes," Juan said.

"And Father Anthony?"

"Yes."

"From our point of view of course this is so unbelievable that we can only presume that you are imagining these contacts consciously, or possibly subconsciously. However, in a file which was never in Father Anthony's hands and which we are certain could never have been in yours, the man Makar Boleslov, to whom Father Anthony thought you were related, describes the method by which he communicated with the dead. As this apparently coincides exactly with the method you use, that is direct cerebral contact, we are interested in investigating the matter a little further. Would you be willing to carry out an experiment or two, under controlled circumstances of our choosing, by which we mean, would you speak to the dead in our presence?"

"Yes," Juan said without hesitation.

"Good," the Bishop said, surprised that everything should be so easy, even a little disappointed perhaps. "We will not, of course, tell you who the deceased is and will request you to ask the departed soul a few special questions as part of the experiment."

"It will not be Father Anthony then?" Juan asked. He had taken it for granted all along that it would be.

"Not for the first experiment."

"When will we experiment?" Juan asked.

"A body has been prepared in the infirmary, I believe, Your Emminence," the Bishop said turning to the Cardinal, "We could proceed whenever you wish."

"Then let us proceed," the Cardinal said, and everyone rose.

Juan had no idea where he was being taken. They all went in single file down yards of corridors.

They first entered a small room in which they were all requested to put on white aprons and gauze masks by two efficient nuns. Then they went into an extremely brightly lit room which smelt strongly of disinfectant and formaldehyde and in the centre of which lay the shape of a corpse under a green plastic sheet on a stainless steel trolley.

On a table was a sophisticated recording machine connected to a microphone set up on a stand close to the body.

The Deacon handed a typed card to Juan. It was a list of questions they wanted him to ask the deceased.

Juan glanced quickly at the questions which were straightforward identity checks, then asked for the head to be uncovered.

A mortician stepped forward, pulled the green plastic sheet back from the face and Juan found himself looking at the peaceful features of a middle aged woman. The eyes were closed, the thin lips tight shut, the hair grey, cut short.

He moved to a position behind the head, leaned forward and placed his forehead against the ice-cold brow. The hiss came instantly. It was as though it were travelling at tremendous speed through a tunnel leading from the infinite, a tunnel into the woman's skull and into his. Then suddenly silence within an echoing void.

"Who am I speaking to?" he asked out loud. His voice sounded young, nervous, in the clinically bright room.

"My name is Sister Teresa."

"Sister Teresa?" he repeated.

He was aware of the surprise around him. If they were surprised at this, how would they react to what might follow?

"When did you die Sister Teresa?" he asked, glancing at the question sheet.

"Ten days ago . . ."

"Ten days ago . . ." he repeated. "Where did you die?"

"I died in the Monastery of Santa Rosalia in Montevideo."

"What was the cause of your death?"

"I died of cancer."

He repeated the answer.

"Can I help you?" he asked. It was his own question.

"I want to be cremated."

He repeated her answer.

"Why do you want to be cremated?"

"They are preserving me . . ." the voice said to him, *"They*

have treated my body for the journey home to bury me in the family vault. I do not want that. I want to be cremated."

There was a silence.

He spoke her words out loud for the benefit of the others, for the tape recorder which was humming quietly to one side.

"Where are you now?"

There was a silence.

"Where are you now?" he asked again.

"I am here . . . with my body . . . within my head . . . Tell my brother he is wrong to have done this to me."

"Who is your brother?" he asked, forgetting to repeat what she had said.

"The Cardinal is my brother. His Emminence Cardinal Gregory of Elba . . ."

The silence that followed was the silence of the end. Juan knew that she was gone, her energy having been used up. He straightened up, wiped his brow, aware that he was perspiring. He also realized how tense everyone else was in the room.

The Bishop, his face creased with concern, looked at him for a long time, then stuttered, "You asked two questions: "Where are you now" and "Who is your brother", but you did not repeat the answers."

"She is within her body, within her skull, and her brother is His Emminence Cardinal Gregory of Elba."

"Of Elba!" The Bishop was unsettled by what could be disrespectful to His Emminence.

"I was born on the Island of Elba," the Cardinal said, stepping forward. "It was a family joke that I should become Cardinal of Elba."

He was sheet white and could not hide the fact that his hands were trembling though he was clasping them tightly.

"I think we owe Brother Juan a few apologies, and should now grant him his wish."

Juan was not sure which wish would be granted, he had so many, but he saw the Bishop nod to one of the morticians, who left the room.

He turned to look at Francesca. She was standing well against the wall, looking at her feet, like everyone else she had fallen silent and paled visibly.

The double doors opened and another body was wheeled in. As with Sister Teresa it was covered by a green plastic sheet and he was not sure who it could be.

"Father Anthony was disintered this morning on the pretext of an autopsy being necessary due to the uncertain circumstances of his death," the Bishop explained.

"If you can convey our apologies . . . ?" the Cardinal said, stepping back.

Juan looked at everyone in turn.

Their attitude towards him had changed, from one of patience with a demented choirboy to one of respect for that which could not be fully understood.

"When I have finished communicating with Father Anthony, I want him cremated. Will you promise that this will be done?" He looked at the Cardinal.

The Cardinal nodded agreement, much to the Bishop's astonishment.

One Deacon crossed himself.

Juan pulled back the plastic sheet and looked at the fearful face. It was creased with pain and sadness and looked a sickly yellow and ugly in death.

He placed his forehead against the jelly-soft brow as he was accustomed to doing, and waited for the tell-tale hiss.

There was nothing for a long time.

Then it came, hard and loud, as though escaping under pressure.

"Father Anthony?"

"You've . . . come . . . back . . ."

"Do you know where you are Father?"

"In my head, Juan . . . I cannot escape . . ."

"I meant your body. Do you know where your body is now?"

"It . . . hardly matters . . . to . . . me."

"You are in the Vatican Father, you have been forgiven, they are even granting you a cremation."

"Do not trust them, Juan . . . they cannot afford to trust you . . ."

Juan hesitated. He had not repeated the answers so far, had not been asked to. It was a private conversation, and he carried on.

"Have you any advice for me. What I should do, where I should go?"

"Leave . . . Lose yourself where you cannot be found. Calixtus may be the answer . . ."

"Calixtus?" Juan repeated out loud. "Is there anything else I can do for you, Father?"

"Fire . . . cremation . . ."

"Is fire the only answer?"

"Yes . . ."

"What of . . . decapitation . . . what of the head severed from the body?"

"It is that which remains in the head's cavity, where the brain cells were that live on as a memory, Juan. Burn the walls of the prison and the human senses escape."

"Is this my duty now . . . to release the senses of the dead so that they may escape for ever?"

"Only if it is a strong desire . . ."

The voice sounded weaker. Juan felt he was going to lose the contact.

"Are you going so soon Father?"

There was no answer.

"Father?" It was already over.

He straightened up slowly, pulled the plastic sheet over the yellowed face and turned to those who were watching him.

"I would like him to be cremated as soon as possible," he said to the Cardinal.

The Cardinal nodded again, drained by what he had seen Juan experiencing.

"Why do you lose contact?" one of the Deacons asked, stepping forward.

"Energy is lost," Juan said.

"Where does the energy come from?"

"I don't know," Juan said. "Perhaps it is stored within us, perhaps generated by me. But I don't know. There are many things I cannot answer because I do not understand them myself."

"May I suggest that we return to your office, Your Emminence?" the Bishop said, opening the doors. "There are many things to be discussed."

As soon as they were all settled in the privacy of the Cardinal's chamber, the Bishop stood up and nervously spoke out against what had been agreed.

"If Father Anthony's remains are to be cremated, Your Emminence, and word goes out that this was permitted by the Vatican, we will have a new movement within our ranks demanding cremation as we did for the clergy to marry. Requests for disinterments will follow, clandestine clubs will be formed and our cemeteries will be raided and the bodies piled high and burned! The crematoriums, always a commercial venture, will fan this, er, fire, and hallowed ground the world over will be desecrated. We have no evidence that what Brother Juan said is true. Granted it was a remarkable piece of showmanship, but it might be due to some psychic capability, telepathy, for example, an ability to read your mind, my mind . . ."

The Cardinal looked at the Bishop patiently and waited for him to calm down, then spoke slowly.

"Father Anthony committed suicide dear Bishop, I don't think we need trouble ourselves with the rights and wrongs of what happens to his remains, they are no longer those of a Roman Catholic."

"Well," said the Bishop, still nervous, "I would propose that we have a council meeting before the request is granted."

The Cardinal closed his eyes and breathed in and out slowly as he considered the Bishop's plea. After a while he opened his eyes and drew himself up in the chair.

"I think that we must study more carefully what took place this afternoon. I would like typescripts of the recordings made and for Brother Juan to write down Father Anthony's answers to the questions he himself asked and which he did not repeat, and I think a special meeting of the council should then be called to decide what can be done, indeed, what must be done. Meanwhile, I suggest that Brother Juan be made comfortable within the Vatican City."

The Cardinal smiled and stood up in a way of dismissing those present.

"Your Emminence," Juan said, standing up with the others, "Before the typescripts are submitted to the committee might I suggest one more experiment? It has been suggested that I might have been reading people's minds, that I might be using telepathy, that I might be doing this subconsciously by tapping other people's thoughts, I do not argue the point, but supposing I were allowed to communicate with the dead of long ago, in the catacombs of Saint Calixtus, for example. Father Anthony suggested the name . . ."

CATACOMB

The Cardinal was a diplomat. Having granted the Bishop his request, it was only fair to grant Juan his.

"Providing recordings and typescripts are made and all is done under your supervision Bishop, yes. I will call the council meeting for one day early next week."

Juan spent that night in a room reserved for special Vatican guests.

Francesca had bid him a sweet goodnight at the door of the Cardinal's chambers before he had been led away to his "guest room." She had pecked him on the cheek, squeezed his wrist secretively as though to tell him that she was on his side, but she had disappeared down the corridor a fraction too quickly, her steps a fraction too sprightly, as though she was relieved that she was finished with an assignment she had never really enjoyed. It had unnerved him badly.

At six the next evening he was asked to join the Bishop and the two Deacons. They were driven to the Catacombs of Saint Calixtus.

Off the Via Appia, just outside the city walls, the catacombs were reached down a tree-lined driveway leading to a number of simple farm buildings, one of which served as entrance to the endless miles of subterranean tunnels used by the Christians to bury their dead in the time of the Romans.

An official guide met them, a small man in a black suit and dog collar, talkative, speaking English with a bad accent and genuflecting to kiss the Bishop's ring.

They went down some steep steps into what seemed like a huge cellar, ill lit by a few dim bulbs. They went into a chapel where a marble statue of a saint by Bellini represented the torment suffered under the Romans at the time of the persecutions. The guide told him about her at length and that her body had supposedly never decayed.

"We have very few bodies left here, of course, two have been preserved under glass which we will be pleased to show you."

One of the Deacons, aware that the man was irritating the Bishop, took him aside to whisper something in his ear, and they were immediately taken down one of the passages flanked by the empty tombs. At the end was a gate which he opened.

"This leads to one of the sepulchres where the bones of Saint Clement of Saforzi are at rest."

The guide shone a torch, for there was no light down this passage, and stopped at a small door which he unlocked.

"We do not show this to the public any more, we used to but were requested to desist after the bones were consecrated and Clement Saforzi was officially recognized as a Saint."

So he was going to make contact with a saint!

The guide opened the heavy door and shone his torch around the rock walls. In the centre on a stone block was a casket with a glass lid.

Inside a skeleton had been laid on red silk. The skull was beautifully preserved, clean and polished as though in a museum.

When the guide had unlocked the casket he was asked to leave the sepulchre, and he did so discreetly, handing his torch to the first Deacon, who lifted the glass lid.

There was no repulsion, no smell, only that of a preserving chemical. The skull seemed to grin up at Juan, grin up at them all.

"May I pick it up?"

The Bishop nodded.

He lifted the skull out of the casket, holding it very carefully, like a precious piece of antique glass, and knelt down on the ground, not for prayer but to concentrate more.

It was then that he realized the whole pantomime was a trick. The skull was not real, it was made of plastic, or some ceramic, but it was not real. The Bishop was trying to catch him out, hoping he would go through his ritual, then disclose the truth, proving that Juan was a charlatan.

It made him angry.

Then he realized that whatever he did they would trap him. Father Anthony had warned him. He should escape, and this was the place to do so.

He closed his eyes, breathed in deeply and pretended to get a contact.

"Clement Saforzi?" Juan said out loud.

"You are Clement Saforzi? You are not . . . Who are you then? Domenico Parto? When did you die? In the year 1465? Did you know you had been canonised? You did not . . . ?"

He suddenly got up, put the skull back in the casket and turned to the Bishop.

"His name is Domenico Parto, he died in 1465, these are not the remains of Clement Saforzi."

"But what you are saying is sacrilegious, these bones have been consecrated," the first Deacon said, incensed.

"What I am saying is as farcical as your attempt to trick me!" Juan said. "These are not real bones."

The Bishop, mortified, turned on his heels and walked out of the sepulchre, followed by the first Deacon.

The second Deacon, not unamused by the developments, put a hand on his shoulder and shook his head.

"Brother Juan, you should not have antagonised him so."

"What will happen now?"

"I expect they will find fault with you and eventually send you to the Monastery of Sao Joao de Baptista."

He had heard of it.

"Where those who do not conform end their days?" Juan said.

"It is a beautiful island, many tourists have tried to buy it and failed. It outshines Mont Saint Michel."

"But it was a prison." He would have to escape. It was now or never.

He would have to wait for a moment of confusion when they made their way out, when he would be able to run in the opposite direction. He had seen lengths of these black tunnels, they were endless, kilometre upon kilometre on four levels, each going deeper down than the other. It could be done, it had to be done.

The guide who had waited for them in the dark passage outside now led the way back, thankful to have his torch. The Bishop followed him, then the first Deacon, Juan and the second Deacon.

Ahead Juan saw a passage to the left. This would be the one, before they started up the stairs leading to the main exit.

As they passed several empty tomb holes and came to the passage, he stopped and said, "Father, I just saw . . . I just saw. . . ."

"What my son?" the first Deacon asked.

"In a tomb back there, two tombs back, a face."

"A face?"

The guide protested. "There is no one down here on this level."

"It was a face with a halo," Juan said.

"A halo my son? Where?"

To the Bishop's irritation the Deacon fussed and started turning back.

Juan waited for the split second when both guide and Bishop had their backs turned, then he dived into the black passage and ran.

CHAPTER
— 10 —

He put his hands out and ran as fast as he could.

It was frightening because it was dangerous, any second he could fall down a hole, hit a completely blank wall, smack his head against something low, but he ran on.

Sensing a space to his right, another passage, he turned down it and stopped for breath. Now he heard the confusion among his pursuers and saw the torch shining.

There were tombs and holes above him, behind him, in front of him. He pulled himself up into one of them, lay down as deeply into it as he could and kept quite still.

They went by. They passed the passage, shone the torch down it, ran on, all four of them. He had lost them, he had escaped immediate discovery.

He stretched his legs out. He was too big for the tomb hole, his head was pressed against the ancient brickwork, his feet touching the other end, his knees bent. There was no smell, only that of dry dust, no feeling of death. It reminded him rather of a compartment he had slept in once on a train journey in Argentina.

He heard voices coming closer now, Italians shouting to each other, quite a number of them.

Systematically a search party would go down every passage and look in every tomb.

He eased himself down and trod the blackness cautiously. He had the time to make his escape good, he had the time to decide where he would go. He was in a labyrinth and sooner or later he would have to get out, but right now he had to get in so deep that no one would be able to find him.

They had all been going up one passage heading for the exit and he had dashed down a tunnel on the left, then he had taken this one on the right. So he would continue the pattern, left then right, left then right. When he wanted to return he would reverse the process, right then left, right then left.

He came to an opening on the left and cautiously went into it. The ground sloped down. He put his hands out, felt the walls on either side. Then there were steps leading down to the lower level, the third, or was it the fourth? No need to fear levels, all he had to do was keep climbing on the return journey.

Suddenly he heard a noise, closer voices.

He started down the steps too quickly, his foot hit something, he lost his balance, realized he was incapable of knowing what to grab hold of, felt himself falling and hit his head hard against a wall.

It hurt. It really hurt. The bruise came up immediately above the right eye. It did not feel sticky, he had not cut himself, but he was stunned, and frightened now. He was on his knees, the ground around him felt sandy. He dug into his pocket remembering the lighter. Francesca's gift. He waited, listened, the sounds had gone. He flicked it.

The flame was dazzling.

He put it out immediately, placed his hand between the lighter and his eyes, then lit it again.

He had fallen about two feet, a hole in the wall, and he

was in a low chamber. Tunnels led off to the right and left. He decided on the right. Left then right, left then right.

He heard the voices again. They were coming down the very passage he had taken. Were his footprints in the dust guiding them to him? He blew out the flame and felt his way to the entrance of the tunnel.

His footfall echoed now, for the first time. He was on rock, or brickwork, different from before, no tombs, just a tunnel leading from one part of the catacombs to another perhaps. Suddenly it ended. No walls, nothing above his head, he was in a void and he stopped dead and listened.

Not a sound. He flicked the lighter.

He was in another chamber, a high one with more alternative tunnels and passages leading off. A noise, a voice echoing, impossible to tell from where. Maybe he was going round in a circle, would find himself facing them.

The prospect of being caught frightened him, spurred him on. He went to the left. There were empty graves now on either side, four high, a long passage of death. He didn't give himself time to think of the shadows that might be around, he could help the dead, they knew that, surely they knew that.

He turned right, happy to be putting distance between himself and his live enemies, then the ground started sloping down again. He flicked his lighter. Steep, a few feet away steps going further down.

The temperature dropped, it was much cooler, he was in the very depths of the catacombs and the tombs were walled in. This was an area which had not been tampered with.

He thought of spiders and stopped dead. Why did he have to think of that? His fear of spiders. He couldn't go on. Ahead he could imagine a cobweb, a huge cobweb and a big hairy spider. The idea was fearful, he flicked on the lighter.

No spider, no cobweb. He would have to overcome this fear. "Think of the jam jar and think of Carmen!" he said out loud to himself.

It had cured him, for a while. It was his aunt's idea, the only good idea she had ever had. He had screamed one night on seeing a spider in the bathroom, and she had been sympathetic for once, she had understood his fear, and she had been very gentle.

"What we will do," she had said, "Is take this spider and put it in a jam jar, feed her and put her on your bookshelf. We will call her Carmen and every morning and every night for a week you will look at her, after which you will never be afraid of spiders again. Trust me Juan, my mother did the same to me. You will get to know her and she will get to know you."

It hadn't worked. Not really. He had been brave, had stared at the ugly creature, but had dreamt of it crawling inside his bed. He had stared at it, talked to it, had fed it dead flies collected from the window sill.

If you wish to live and thrive, Let the spider run alive . . .

He stopped, sensed something ahead. He flicked on the lighter and found himself facing another wall. He was at a T-junction.

To the left or right? He had forgotten. Then the lighter flame dimmed and went out. He worked the flint. Nothing. He shook the lighter, got a flame for two seconds, then it dimmed and went out.

Oh God! Four levels down and lost. He turned round. He would go no further. He would try and find his way back. But which way had he come? Left, right, left, right? Had he taken the left or the right last? How could he have forgotten? Was it Carmen seeking vengeance now?

If you wish to stay alive . . .

He had killed her. Opened the top of the jar one night

and sprayed her with a fly killer. She had instantly shrivelled up, become minute, her long hairy legs curling. Then he had taken the jar and hurled it out of the window. His aunt had never mentioned it again and other fears had taken over. The ghosts, the hauntings. Well, Carmen could send her friends to attack him now, he was vulnerable and on the point of panic. Carmen, or the dead.

"Keep moving!" he said to himself.

He came to a passage, to the right. If he could see he might remember. He had come down a long tunnel of tombs, but had that been before or after the steps down?

He walked slowly, feeling the tomb holes on either side and then he stubbed his toe on a step. He put his hand out. It was a wall.

He followed it around. He was in another chamber.

He made his way round, sometimes closing his eyes, sometimes not, it made no difference, he could not see. There was air, there was air coming from somewhere but then that was the marvel of the catacombs, the ventilation. He went round once and round again. He could not find the way out. He could not find the way he had come in!

He crouched down, on his haunches, hugged his knees. "Do not panic Juan. You are an intelligent boy and you have friends among the dead. Do not panic. Just think things out carefully."

What was it that Father Anthony had said . . . ? It is because the young see everything as it is and feel everything exactly as it is that they survive madness. He wasn't sure it was true. He moved to a corner and felt the wall. There was a loose brick to one side. He eased it out, making a loud scraping noise. For the first time he became aware of the silence, became aware of his own breathing. He pulled the brick out and put it down on the ground in the corner. He then started moving to the right, along one wall, one corner, along the next wall, another corner, along the third wall, the third corner, along the fourth wall, and his brick!

How could that be? How could he be enclosed now, unless they had guessed where he was and rapidly, silently, walled him in.

Imagine being walled in. And a real fear overcame him. Was this not exactly what death was, to be enclosed in total darkness with no communication. Was he dead? Had he fallen down a hole and killed himself without realizing it? Was he dead, suddenly, and like all the others, incarcerated within his own skull?

He had of course only felt the walls at shoulder level, he had only put his hands out straight in front of him. He went round again, quickly, wall one, wall two, his hands feeling the whole wall, top and bottom. Wall three.

He found a gap, a hole, an exit just below chest level. He had been crouching as he walked then, had bent double and had passed into this chamber through the hole without realizing it.

Then, as he got down on his hands and knees to crawl through, he felt the presence. A few feet behind him, it was there. It gave out no light, made no sound, but it was there, trying to stop him leaving. He crawled through the hole quickly, stood up and moved in a straight line, trailing his fingers on either side. Then his foot again hit something.

He put out his hand—another wall. Was he back at the T-junction where his lighter had run out? And the panic set in. His mouth went dry, his stomach was curling in on itself with fear. He was thirsty, he wanted to go to the lavatory.

He couldn't bear that. He couldn't bear the idea of being imprisoned without food or water and soiling himself in the dark, even death would not have those discomforts.

He took some deep breaths to help him remain calm, and

became aware that the air was no longer fresh, no longer cool. It was musty.

He crouched down, hugged his knees, balanced himself on the balls of his feet. No sounds, nothing, he was alone in a grave deep beneath the surface of the earth. This is exactly what it was like to be dead: total obscurity, lights only in the head, imagination rolling around, memories to go over which got lost in confusion, and the knowledge of eternity, of nothing, no communication.

He started to hum a Gregorian chant. How long would the dead remember music? How long would they be able to sing themselves to sleep? But there was no sleep. No sleep, eternal awakening in a void, until someone like him came to the rescue once in a million years.

Where were they, his haunting spirits, now that he needed them? He retraced his steps. He crawled back through the low opening and into the chamber where he had felt the presence.

Had they led him down here? Had they all guided him down here, for what? To kill him? What good would that do? Didn't they understand that he was powerless to do what they wished without help, human, live help? He had tried, had he not?

Or were they leading him to power, somehow?

He turned to the left, found the corner with his brick, moved his hand upwards, stood up, felt for the hole where the brick had come from and removed others, one, two, three, a whole lot of bricks came out.

He was breaking open a tomb, feeling around in the cavity. There was a great deal of dust, then he touched what he had been hoping to find . . . a bone.

It was a thigh bone. He moved his fingers along it to the hip bone, the ribs, the jaw bone, the teeth. He felt around, the dome of the forehead, the eye holes, dry. He pulled out the skull, the whole of the skull and felt it in the dark, felt the brittleness of the bone.

He was with death, but somehow for him this death was now his friend. He raised the skull to his forehead, pressed the dome against his brow. The hiss sounded far off, but it was there, very faint, very faint. It increased. He leaned back against the wall and slid down to sit on his haunches, holding the skull close to his forehead. The hissing gathered speed, was travelling towards him, expanding, a deep sound within himself, between his ears, like the noises in a dream.

The sound stopped, the person was there, right there in his own head. Then he saw something quite fearful. A few feet from him a thin line of light started to pulsate. It was a foot long or so, vertical and as it grew in intensity he realized he was looking at the materialization of a spinal chord.

It was pulsating more rapidly and ribs began to appear like branches growing out of a tree, then a faintness round the thighs, the arms, whispy legs, then the head, whiter, not giving off light, not shining, but appearing like the clear shadow in a negative print. It had dark eyes, a mouth which moved, masticating, and hair, long white hair.

"Who are you?" he whispered, still holding the brittle skull to his forehead.

"I'll lead you out of here and to freedom if you promise to release me," the voice said in his head. *"You must crush my skull and disintegrate every part of it to dust and cast it to the winds."*

"I promise," he whispered, "I promise."

"Hold me as you are holding me now and don't let go..."

The apparition glided slowly towards him, hesitated a moment then quite suddenly sucked itself into him.

For a terrible moment he was paralysed by an icy grip in every one of his limbs, and then he felt himself moving, felt his own muscles moving, his legs walking though he was

CATACOMB

in no way controlling them. He was now an unconnected brain in his own body being moved by another being.

There was light now as well, and people. People standing, people crouching, people asleep in the candlelit passages that he was moving through. Some made way for him, some he brushed against. They were hairy people with beards, clothed in rags, thin with swollen bellies many of them, there were children, and there was a hum, a constant hum of conversation he did not understand.

He went up some steps. Oil lamps were burning now. He turned down more corridors filled with people, entered a chamber where people were munching fruit. Most looked frightened, sickly. In the tomb holes there were bodies wrapped in linen, on the floor were dying people, some mutilated, blood caked on stumps which had been arms, the mushroom growth of gangrene bubbling on sores.

Up more steps, there was less light, fewer candles, fewer oil lamps, fewer people, younger people, younger men with weapons, with knives, one with a sword.

He was moving through the past, he was being moved through the apparition's past, through the catacombs with their Christian ghosts hiding from persecution.

Suddenly there was blackness, as though an electric cable had been yanked out of him. Deep blackness and no sounds at all.

He had lost the contact and had no idea where he was. He remained quite still, did not move for fear of falling into a pit ahead, or cracking his head against a beam, a wall.

"Are you there?" he said in the dark.

There was no answer.

He cautiously took the skull away from his forehead and waited.

Now he saw a dimness, a vague light ahead, and he moved forward again, taking one careful step at a time till he reached a tunnel, a long tube of a hole with a pinpoint of light at the end.

He got down on his hands and knees and crawled down it, holding the skull in one hand.

It was damp. He was afraid of worms now, and spiders again, he was getting back to the land of the living, and the land of the living was wet and uncomfortable. Perhaps he preferred the dryness, the brittleness of ancient bones to the rotting of live earth.

He reached a stream of water running across the tunnel, he crossed it, getting his knees wet, then the ground rose steeply till he reached an opening into a cave.

There was much more light now, and he could see the shapes of the rocks around and above him. He still had to crawl, but he made his way towards the light source, turned a little, followed a worn path. The light brightened slowly, then suddenly he was out in the open—he was right out in the open and it was night time.

The light that he had seen so brightly was the night sky with a faint moon behind clouds. Had it been day he would have seen the exit a long time before, perhaps on many occasions he might have seen his way about.

He breathed in the fresh air, he breathed in and held the skull up to have a look at it.

It was small, a half skull, no jaw, he pressed it against his forehead and waited.

Nothing. Had the contact been broken for ever? Had the fresh air already started a deterioration? He pressed it a little with his fingers, and they went through and it broke up like a swallow's nest. He felt the dust between his fingers, then took the pieces and crushed them between his hands, pulverized the skull. It was so easy, so delicate, so brittle, he felt the dust in his hands and held it up to the breeze and saw it disappear into the air.

"As promised," he said, out loud.

He had no idea where he was. Certainly there were no lights around, no houses visible, but he was on the side of a hill and figured that Rome might be round the other slope.

With his eyes accustomed to the night he saw a path, white against the darker grass around it. He went down it, aware that somewhere in the bushes or hidden among the trees his Vatican enemies might be waiting for him. But somehow he felt safe. He was no longer alone, he had been helped, albeit in the most nightmarish fashion, and he had been able to release one mind from the imprisonment of burial.

What of all those people in the cemeteries throughout the world, had the Bishop been right in prophecying a madness to cremate? And why had iron-age man incinerated his dead, surely not only for health reasons? And why did the Brahmins cremate on the banks of the Ganges? Were some religions better informed about the after life?

The path went down steeply, then levelled out and he was on a track leading to a little building to the left: signs of civilization. Who would believe what world he had just left?

He heard the purr of a car travelling at speed, saw the leaves of the trees shine silver when caught in the light of the headlamps. There was a road nearby then, he would make for that, and guess the direction he should go in.

The track eventually led to a main road which was narrow and cobbled and very straight. The Via Appia, he was sure. From Rome to Brindisi. He started along it, deciding that the city must be to the left because there were more lampposts in that direction.

As he reached the first one he saw that his suit was filthy, his shirt brown with dust, his shoes caked in mud.

He smelt his hands, the tips of his fingers. They were

earthy, nothing more. The dead, after a thousand years, did not smell.

A car came tearing down the middle of the road going the wrong way, its tyres purring on the cobbles.

He flattened himself against the endless wall. It was a long dangerous road.

Later, another car came whistling past in the right direction. He stuck out his thumb, made a signal, but did not really expect anyone would stop at such speed.

There was no harm trying. He walked on, happy to be in the cool fresh air of the night. He was a survivor. He was also a little hungry and thirsty. After all, he had only been down in the catacombs four or five hours perhaps, it was probably about midnight.

A car with yellow lights was coming along the road more slowly. He waved at it, thumbed it. A large woman with blonde hair and a cigarette in the corner of her mouth stopped and opened the door for him.

"*Roma?*" he asked.

"*Si. Ividamente.*"

He got in. The car smelt of her scent, a heavy perfume and of dogs. There were two of them on the back seat, large Afghans, their four startled eyes staring at him.

She said something to him in Italian which he didn't understand.

"*No comprendo. Lo siento,*" he said in Spanish, then, "I am South American."

"So," she said, "We can speak in English."

"Oh, *you're* American," he said, relieved.

She had a strong Italian accent but spoke with a drawl.

"I used to be. One of my husbands was a U.S. Marine. So, what is a pretty boy like you doing out this time of night in the wilds? You ought to be at home in bed with someone."

"What is the time please? I have no idea."

"The time, sonny, is one a.m."

"Oh . . . I got lost. I was visiting the catacombs and got lost on my way out."

"The catacombs? A morbid little boy are we?" And she squeezed his leg, rather painfully. She had hands and fingers of steel.

"Have you lived in Rome long?" he asked politely.

"Are you making conversation, or do you really want to hear my life story?"

"I don't mind," he said, amused. She was very direct and forceful.

"You tell me yours first and then I'll tell you mine," she suggested.

He wasn't sure what to tell her. She didn't strike him as someone who would frequent the Vatican council, but you could never tell.

"I'm a student," he said.

"Of life? What do you study?"

"Latin and Greek."

"Oh, right up my street. In my business I use Latin and Greek all the time!" Her laugh came from well behind her throat.

"What is your business?" he asked.

"I am a whore, sweetheart. I am a Madame. I run a brothel just outside Rome, but tonight I am going to comb the streets of the sinful city for some more girls because my customers are getting bored with what I have to offer. They need new blood. You wouldn't like to come and work for me? You're very pretty."

"But I'm a boy!" He wasn't shocked, more surprised by the suggestion.

"Exactly. We could dress you up as a girl and surprise

the customers. They would love that. I pay very well, 50,000 lire a throw." She squeezed his leg again.

He wanted to get out, was afraid of getting involved in something he couldn't handle, didn't understand.

"You're really a very attractive young man. Have you a girl friend?" she asked.

"Yes."

"What does she do, study Latin and Greek too?"

"She works for the Vatican," he said truthfully.

"That figures."

They drove on in silence till she had to slow right down. Ahead were a line of policemen and fire engines with their blue lights flashing.

"Your catacombs have perhaps caught fire," she said lightly, "That is the entrance to them there."

Had the police been called out to look for him, then?

It would be too much of a coincidence. He slid down in the seat cautiously, but the car was waved on.

"Where do you want to go?" the woman asked, stubbing out her cigarette in an overflowing ashtray.

"Home."

"And where is that?"

He hesitated too long. He didn't want to tell her Francesca's address, didn't even want to go there, and he didn't know anywhere else.

"You've nowhere to go, have you? I don't think you are a scholar at all, I think you are on the make. Come on, come back with me, once I've picked up these girls."

He said nothing. They were outside the city walls now turning in through one of the arches.

"When did you last have a feed?" she went on.

"A little while ago."

"Hungry?"

"I'm thirsty," he admitted.

"So we'll stop and have a feed and you can tell me the truth about yourself. OK?"

He was lost now, in a quarter of Rome he did not know.

She bumped the car onto the pavement in way of parking and got out.

She had once been attractive. She wore a tight black silk dress that reminded him of his aunt's chemise, and a bright pink boa. She had heavy costume jewellery hanging round her neck which might have been the real thing, and very high heeled shoes.

"Right, my darling," she said to him, "Take my arm or I'll be accosted."

He took her arm. He was slightly taller than her, but felt smaller, and people, he was aware, looked at them both because they were obviously a very strangely matched couple.

When they came into the brightness of the cafes she suddenly looked at him and his suit.

"Sweetheart, where have you been? You're very dusty. Have you been rolling around on the grass? Come in and get tidied up."

She pulled him up some grand red carpeted steps into a palace of a hotel lobby and led him straight down a corridor to the washroom.

Though the door was clearly marked "Signore," she marched him in and pushed him towards the uniformed attendant.

"Mario, tidy this little boy up for me, we're meeting a producer and he doesn't look too new. Dust him down and find him a clean shirt."

Mario took him into a marble hall which was the toilet and asked for his coat, his trousers, his shirt and his shoes.

Juan took them off obediently, washed his hands, his face, combed his hair and was handed a clean towel.

It was good, the refreshing water, the soap. How had he

moved from the catacombs of death to the centre of the *dolce vita* in Rome so quickly?

Mario eventually returned, found him, gave him his suit, brushed, neat, clean, a new light blue shirt, a likeable patterned tie and his shoes, shiny black.

He got dressed quickly, looked at himself in the mirror and was rather pleased with the effect. The tie made a lot of difference, it made him look elegantly serious.

"That's better," the woman said when he joined her in the lobby. "Now I can be quite proud of you."

"What is your name?" he asked.

"My name is Messalina, my darling, but I am also known as Framboise. We'll sit here and feed you," she said, settling down at an empty cafe table, "And then we must do the clubs. I'm looking for a particularly delicious girl called Lola."

He had a plate of fettuccini, another dish with grilled prawns, a glass of wine which he drank slowly after gulping down some iced water. She just had a cognac and watched him with interest.

"You haven't eaten for days, have you?"

"I ate this morning!"

"Where?"

He hesitated too long again. But how could he tell her he had had lunch in the Vatican as a guest of a Cardinal?

"You're beginning to intrigue me. There is something too secretive about you, which I like. You're being cautious, and that is good. But you are afraid of something. The police? Are you in trouble with the police? You can tell me."

"No," he said.

"I was fifteen when the Americans came and liberated Rome. I am the original type of girl they made so many movies about. I turned whore, married three times, was successful with one husband because he died, and bought myself a farmhouse which is now the best brothel in the country. I know everyone and everyone knows me. More important, I know their vices. I can probably help you if you will let me."

She brought a gold cigarette box out of her deep handbag, picked out a cigarette, tapped it twice on the flat of the lid, stuck it in her mouth, and lit it.

"So what's your story? I think that you could do a little singing for your supper."

She timed the request just as the waiter brought him a huge gelati, several coloured ice creams piled on top of each other, covered with a thick chocolate sauce and topped with a cherry.

"If I told you you wouldn't believe me."

"Why would I not believe you? Last night I had a client who requested a decorated melon with a hole in it!"

He had no idea what she was talking about.

"He did not want a girl, he wanted to seduce a melon. We carved this hole in it the size of an average you-know-what, stuck diamond earrings into it, put a diamond tiara on top of it, then one of my girls sat down holding it between her legs and the man seduced the melon. He was very happy. Now tell me your story."

"I can talk to the dead," Juan said straight out.

The wine had gone to his head, he knew it, he knew he should not have said anything.

She looked at him for a long time in silence, studying him. "Waiter," she said, "have you a copy of this morning's newspaper?"

The waiter said he'd go and have a look.

She ordered another drink, put her elbows on the table and stared at him some more.

"Occasionally in my life extraordinary things have happened to me. A chance meeting with someone, picking up a wallet full of money, winning a lottery, marrying a rich man who dies a month later, things like that have happened to me and every time I think it is providence that has had a hand in it. Do you ever get that feeling?"

"No . . ." he said honestly.

She sipped her drink, poured out a little more wine for him and took a long puff at her cigarette.

He knew he should not drink the wine, but it was good, cool, he liked the bitter sweet taste.

The waiter returned with a creased copy of the newspaper. Messalina stuck the cigarette in the corner of her mouth, opened up the pages and scanned the inside spreads. She had to look through the paper twice before finding what she wanted. She then folded the paper so that she could read it.

"You don't understand Italian?"

"No," he said.

"Listen to this, then. The headline reads 'CHOIR BOY LOST IN CATACOMBS. Juan Ramirez Montoneros, a guest choir boy at the Vatican from Argentina, was missing yesterday in the Catacombs of Saint Calixtus when he went off on his own. Catacomb officials have been searching since yesterday morning but fear he may have ventured into the dangerous uncharted lower level and met with a fatal accident. Juan Ramirez claimed that he wanted to talk to the dead and was, according to the official Vatican newspaper *L' Osservatore Romano,* under medical attention.' In other words they think you're a nut."

"What date is that newspaper?" Juan asked, bewildered.

"Today's. That is, yesterday's, because it is now past one in the morning."

"What is today then, what day of the week?"

"Friday, the 26th."

"But I went into the catacombs on Tuesday evening."

"Which could explain why you are so hungry, my friend." She was very casual about it all, did not register any particular surprise.

"But that's incredible, being down there all that time," he said.

"*Did* you communicate with the dead?" she asked, lightly.

"Yes," Juan said, thinking about the skull he had carried through the maze of tunnels, his walk among the people down there, his journey into the past.

"What did they say to you, the dead, how did they behave?"

"They helped me find my way out."

CHAPTER
— 11 —

"What I think we should do now is go and talk to Anastasio Orsini."

"Who is he?" Juan asked.

"He owns an international news magazine or two, a television company or two, a politician or two, he is a Count and a refined Italian aristocrat. He would be interested in meeting you."

It was a more select part of Rome than he had ever been in before. The streets were tree-lined avenues, there was a feeling of space, of freshness, the houses were huge.

Again Messalina parked as though her car were a bulldozer. She pushed open the glass and wrought-iron portals of an elegant mansion and he followed her across a courtyard with a fountain in the middle. To the left was another glass and wrought-iron door with a polished panel of security bell-buttons. She pressed one of them and waited.

It was three in the morning now.

Eventually a deep voice answered: "Si?"

"Messalina," the woman said. "I have something important for you."

There was a buzz and the glass door jumped open.

They walked in, across a carpeted marble floor to a glass

and wrought-iron elevator. They went up in luxurious silence to the third floor, then down a long corridor at the end of which was an open door.

Standing just inside it was a huge man, really tall, really fat, in a peacock blue dressing gown smoking a cigar. He had a mass of untidy grey hair, bushy grey eyebrows and smelt oppressively of lavender.

His eyebrows lifted dramatically. "A present?" he said, looking at Juan delightedly. "You bring me a present? Come in, come in!" His gestures were as grand as his apartment.

Juan had never seen anything like it, not even in Buenos Aires where his family had seldom associated with people poorer than themselves.

It was all tiled marble, black and white, green and white, white walls hung heavy with magnificent tapestries. There was a lion's skin on the floor, as well as Persian carpets, a suit of armour, a huge modern painting against one wall, a ceramic mural, beautiful drapes, statues, chandeliers. A very rich man's home.

"May I introduce you to Juan Ramirez Montoneros, the boy from the Catacombs," Messalina said.

"The boy from the Catacombs! That explains his strange smell. Bonjour mon petit. Do we speak English?"

"Yes sir, and Spanish."

"Spendid, an international boy from the Catacombs. How did you find him?"

"He was thumbing a lift as I was coming in to replenish my cellars with new wine," Messalina said sitting down on a wide velvet couch.

"Sit down Juan, sit down and tell me all," the large man said. "Are you hungry or did she have the decency to feed you? A drink perhaps? A Coca Cola, or has she already corrupted you with wine?"

"I am sure he would like a drink to play with," Messalina said.

"Mmm. You are a choir boy I believe?" Orsini said, eyeing him from below the bushy eyebrows while he poured out a drink of something in a very tall glass.

"No sir."

"You are not? But the papers said . . . but then the papers do lie. Not my papers of course."

"No," Messalina said.

"My editors would have checked. But then if you were lost in the Catacombs I suppose they couldn't get hold of you. How did you find your way out?"

Juan hesitated. The man was amusing. Both were the first amusing people he had met for years. For years and years and years. He risked it.

"I asked someone, sir."

"You *asked* someone? Were there many people to ask down there?"

"Yes sir, quite a few."

"Dead, of course?"

"Yes sir."

"Beautiful! Quite beautiful Messalina. What sort of price are you asking?"

"The usual. Whatever you would pay your stringer for such a story, plus a percentage of international syndications."

"It could be big. It could be enormous if handled properly of course. The point is, how genuine is he?"

"I have no idea. I thought *you* would find out."

"Well, if one is to believe what one hears, he is pretty genuine. You have a very pretty lady friend," Orsini said.

Juan did not understand.

"Another lady in his life?" Messalina said, "I thought I would be enough."

"A sweet ingenue, not at all corruptible, works in the Vatican Press Office. It was she who released the story unofficially two days ago thus forcing the *Osservatore* to print the statement. This young gentleman is apparently a great embarrassment to our Holy friends. He has apparently really talked to the dead! Have you not?"

"Yes sir."

"How frightening," Messalina said.

"What is death, according to those with whom you have spoken who have passed away?" Orsini asked, sitting down close to him.

"It depends, sir. It depends on how you die and how your remains are disposed of."

"Let us say . . . I died and was buried in a huge black marble mausoleum encrusted with gold, a bust of myself on the facade flanked by Doric collonades . . . ?"

"The surroundings don't matter much, sir. The mind however remains captive in the skull until the bones disintegrate. Therefore the more you are protected the longer your mind will live on. The embalmed Egyptians, I should imagine, are still alive in this state."

"What of cremation?"

"Instant release of the mind, sir."

"So you are anti-burial and pro-cremation?"

"I suppose so, sir."

"That will please the Pope if it gets out! What if one is decapitated, one's head chopped off for instance, where would Marie Antoinette be now, for example?"

"I don't know, sir. It depends what was done with her head."

"Is the body not important to the mind, then?"

"No sir. When I . . . when I got help from this person in the catacombs, I carried the remains of the skull into the open, there it fell apart in my hands and the mind was released."

"He's so charming as well, Messalina. A gift from the Gods . . . Ah!" Orsini shouted, looking upwards, "What of God? Have you spoken to him?"

"God does not exist as I was taught it in the church, sir. God is a system, an overall pattern, an energy-field of collected intelligence, but it does not control us, nor is there any judgement on its part."

"A system, no judgement, no God! The Vatican will collapse and will have to sell all those beautiful properties all over the world. I wonder if I should speak to Cardinal Gregory before I make a move. This could have such interesting political repercussions."

"Do you know Cardinal Gregory, sir?" Juan asked, surprised that his name should be mentioned.

"Of course. Do you?"

"Yes, sir. His Emminence was to call a council meeting to decide whether I should be put away. Which is why I escaped while I could."

"Is that so? Is that really so? Have you not got a little something on the Cardinal, Messalina?"

"Unfortunately no. His brother however . . ."

"Ah! His brother. The Cardinal's brother is in the government, which would not easily suffer another scandal. It *would* be a scandal Messalina?"

"It could be."

Juan had the impression he might be in the presence of another Machiavelli.

"Well now, what are we going to do? We have here a young man who claims that he can talk to the dead, that the dead talk back to him. I believe him, thousands will not . . . so we must make sure that thousands do. What are your plans Juan?"

"I have none, sir."

"Your ambitions then?"

"I would like to talk to my mother sir, and my father."

"Where is your mother?"

"She died when I was born, sir."

"Brilliant! He can even write his own copy. Where was she buried? Or was she cremated?"

"She lies in the Calvary Cemetery in New York."

"New York! Imagine. The Americans will love him! We don't start here, we fly him to the States and conquer the New World first. Have you been to New York?"

"Yes sir. I was born there, then I went to Buenos Aires and then to the Monastery of Trasimeno near Florence."

"I think I may look after this story myself," Orsini said, "I think it is too delicate to be trusted to Meloy, though Cadogan would be sensitive to the frailty of all this. It's a question of whether I have the time and the energy really, isn't it?"

He crossed the room, sat down at an ornate desk and flicked through his diary.

"What do you think, Messalina? Do you think the denial of God is more important than lunch with that wonderful new actress who happens to be the Foreign Minister's mistress? Before I cancel a number of important dates Juan, I think I must have some proof myself that you are not a charlatan. What would you suggest we do?"

"His Emminence the Cardinal presented me with a corpse about whom I knew nothing sir, but he knew quite a lot. Would a similar experiment satisfy you?"

"Of course. Gruesome, unwholesome, but an excellent idea. Let us do that. It is now past three in the morning, my first appointment is at ten, with my masseur, which I will give up to no one. Say eleven? You join me for breakfast and I will tell you what arrangements have been made."

"Yes sir."

He rang a bell-pull, summoning Cyprien, a sleepy-eyed manservant who showed Juan to a luxurious bedroom.

Breakfast, served the next morning in a large dining room green with potted plants, was silent.

Juan sat at one end of a long table and Orsini sat at the other reading through a pile of international newspapers, a red telephone at his elbow.

Juan said nothing after his polite "Good morning," was ignored, and tried to munch his toast with as little noise as possible. In the presence of this man he felt small, very young, vulnerable and stupid.

The telephone rang, Orsini picked up the receiver.

Juan couldn't follow the conversation. As he hung up, Orsini acknowledged Juan's presence with a genuine and winning smile. "No one else has picked up the story," he said, "Four lines in *La Stampa*, which I do not own, have died a death, no one is making any comments at the Catacombs, which have re-opened to the public, and the Vatican is pretending to ignore the incident altogether. So, world wide, and nationally, you are forgotten. We are therefore free to resurrect you."

The door opened and Cyprien made way for an earnest young man in a check shirt, jeans and sneakers.

"This is Cadogan, a fellow Americano from California who is going to look after you. Is all set?"

"All is set," Cadogan said, smiling at Juan nervously.

"Good," Orsini said.

Cadogan put his arm round Juan's shoulders and led him out as Orsini sat down to light his first cigar of the day.

Cadogan led Juan to a plain, cream coloured van, parked at the back of Orsini's mansion.

"Get in the back," Cadogan said. "There are blankets and cushions. Just lie down."

When in Rome do as the Romans—Cadogan drove like a madman. After a half-hour drive out of the city he slowed down and turned in through some gates. Juan, kneeling and peeping out of the window, saw they were entering an estate surrounded by tall yellow walls. Ahead was an ornate building and he wondered whether it was Orsini's country palace. Then he saw the gates being closed behind them by two men in white orderly tunics and for a second was afraid that they were going to shut him up in an asylum for good.

The van stopped.

"O.K. There's an open door right here, just get out of the van quickly and go through. We haven't been followed, but let's still play it safe."

Cadogan opened the back doors, Juan slipped out and went straight into the building which smelt strongly of polish and ether.

"What is this place?" he asked.

"It's a private clinic. This way."

They went into what seemed like a consulting room, with a black leather couch, a desk, armchairs and glass cases with surgical instruments.

Juan sat down in one of the armchairs, a little nervous now. "What are we doing? What's going to happen?"

"We're waiting for Orsini, and then see what you can do."

Cadogan started pacing the room, even more nervously than Juan felt. "If your act's convincing, this could be built up into a big story, a really big story. He's going to spend quite a bit on it, the promotion budget surprised me."

The door opened and Orsini came in with a nurse and a man in a white coat. "Right, let's get on with it. I have a lunch date!"

The man in the white coat led the way down to the basement and opened a thick padded door into a cold room. He switched on three bare bulbs hanging over three long kitchen tables on one of which lay a corpse covered with a white sheet.

Orsini went up to the sheet and whipped it off revealing the body of a semi-nude middle-aged woman. For a moment Juan thought it might be his mother, a lunatic idea, but the woman on the slab looked like he had always imagined his mother would.

She wore a bikini bottom, her nails were long, painted red, her face made up, her hair well arranged. Her feet were veined, the toes rather stubby and disjointed suggesting that she had worn tight shoes too often.

"How do you go about making the contact, Juan?"

Juan explained.

"And then what?"

"Then I ask questions."

"Can you ask a few on my behalf?"

"Of course."

"I had some typed out."

Like the Cardinal, Orsini handed him a piece of paper. There were a number of questions on it which Juan decided he would run through in good time.

He took up his position behind the dead woman's head and leaned forward and down.

"Do you want the lights out or anything special?"

"Nothing, thank you."

Juan pressed his brow against the ice-cold forehead and closed his eyes. He was aware of noises that the others in the room were making. Orsini's wheezing, the nurse's starched cuffs brushing against her apron. A cough.

The hiss came within seconds from not too far, like a subway train pushing the air before it in the tunnel.

"Hallo?" he said, hating this moment when he had to make the first contact.

Was he concentrating enough? He had certainly become more confident, was not worried now that nothing would happen.

"Are you there?" he asked.

"*Hi...*" came back the voice. It was a deep voice, a rather mannish voice. "*Who are you?*" it asked.

"Juan Ramirez Montoneros," he answered.

"*My name is George, but they used to call me Kate. I am dead now.*"

He was unsettled, was not sure what the voice was, the humour in it reminded him of Messalina.

"Are you a man or a woman?"

"*Both my darling. I had the operation.*"

"The operation?"

"*You sound very young. How old are you?*"

"Seventeen."

There was a silence.

"I've come to help you," Juan said.

"*Oh you can't do that. This is what I wanted. This is what I hoped for. Eternal time to think. Did they tell you, I did it myself. My choice.*"

"No . . ."

"*I couldn't stand it anymore, the false admiration, the desire for the woman I was not.*"

"You don't want to be released?"

"*No . . .*"

Juan glanced sideways at the questionnaire he was holding. "Could you tell me your full name?"

"*George Hoffman. German stock.*"

"Where were you born?"

"*Connecticut. U.S. of A.*"

"When did you come to Rome?"

"*1976.*"

"What did you do as a profession?"

"*I was a dancer, sweetheart, a great dancer only no one recognized it.*"

"Do you have regrets?"

"*No. I like it here. Suicides probably do. That's what suicides want you see, total anonymity and no sense of time and no responsibility. I can know so many things I would never have known, it's all here, it's like a library, knowledge, you think of the question and know the answer.*"

"Do you have the answer to everything?"

"*I guess so.*"

"Do you know where my father is?" Juan asked.

"*Oh no. I can't know things about you. I can only know things that concern me. It's a very ego-orientated place.*"

"What of the future?"

"*Meaningless.*"

Juan glanced at the questionnaire again. "Do you remember the name of your doctor?"

"*Of course.*"

"What was it?"

"*Doctor Brainsbrook.*"

"And who paid for the operation?"

"*Lorenzo Canachi.*"

"Did he bring you over from the States?"

"*Sure.*"

"Do you know where he went to?"

"*Porto Alegre, Brazil. Don't they all go to Brazil? I was to join him there but it was over.*"

"Are you sure you want to remain where you are?"

"*It's what I've longed for all my life . . . I will disintegrate eventually and go into the next stage. I want time before that. I want time to think and analyze where I went wrong. That is why we are here you see, cremation is fearful for it is as quick as modern living, it is not natural, we need the time to ponder, however painful . . ."*

"What colours can you see?"

"No colours."

"Is it light or dark?"

"Your questions mean nothing."

"You are in a void?"

"If you like."

"Is it frightening?"

"It is beautiful."

And the voice started fading.

"Can you make contact with anyone else?" Juan asked. There was no answer. No answer at all.

"Are you there?" he asked. He knew instinctively the contact had gone. "He's gone," Juan said to those present.

"He's gone?" Orsini said raising his eyebrows.

"It was a man, his name was George Hoffman, he said he had an operation."

Orsini knew. That had been the test. He had been in a monastery, had no idea men could become women with breasts, but Orsini knew.

"Can you remember the other answers?"

Juan reeled them off, his birthplace, when he had come to Rome, the doctor's name, Lorenzo Canachi, Brazil.

"Brazil?" Orsini repeated. "Any particular part of Brazil?"

"Porto Alegre."

"Well my dears, we not only have the find of the century here, we have the find of the millenium. Not since Jesus Christ . . . would you say?" Orsini was beaming.

"Who is Lorenzo Canachi?" Juan asked.

"Canachi? He was the power behind the last Prime Minister, had things going his way till it was discovered that he had made his millions by shipping adolescents to the world's most sinful cities. An ogre and a thief as well as a politician."

The nurse opened the door.

"What are you going to do with him . . . her?" Juan asked.

"What do you mean?"

"What are you going to do with the body now?"

"Bury it I suppose. What do you do with the body?" he asked the doctor.

"You *must* bury her," Juan said. "He must be buried." He was surprised at his own intensity, at his insistence, and he was even more surprised at everyone's reaction, for suddenly there was a respect.

"Whatever you wish," the doctor said.

Orsini himself was actually polite. "Would you mind travelling back to my apartment in the van? I will accompany you this time."

They climbed into the van, Orsini wheezing. "You are not going to be immensely rich, Juan," Orsini said as Cadogan drove off, "You are going to be the richest and the most powerful man on earth. Now you are intelligent enough to realize that this may set you quite a number of problems, not the least of which will be your responsibility to others. Fortunately you have had a very humble upbringing, and you do not seem to be greedy. What I propose to do is to legalize everything and suggest that I become your business adviser. If you trust me."

"I think I can trust you," Juan said. "You seem to be very rich already, so why would you want to be richer?"

"Do not go by appearances. Much may not have been entirely paid for."

"But you have all you need?"

"No. One gets excited by the unexpected and wants it. Right now you are the best gift I have ever had. What you must understand is that you will be in a certain amount of danger."

"Why?"

"You are going to upset history, beliefs, everything the world has been brought up on. It's not a question of upsetting an apple cart, it is a question of you turning humanity inside out, and that will be dangerous for many, many people." Orsini stared at him all the way into Rome, like a child not believing his luck at Christmas.

"When Messalina brought you round last night I liked you enough already, but now!" He sighed. "The saddest thing is that I will never dare touch you!"

"We're here," Cadogan said over his shoulder.

And they got out of the van and went straight into the now familiar house where a woman secretary was waiting for them.

"They're suspecting something. Two of them are out front," she said as they went up in a service lift.

"Then we must get him out of Rome as quickly as possible."

CHAPTER
— 12 —

Orsini had made all the arrangements, elaborate and dramatic, as was his style. They had dyed his hair and smuggled him out of Rome on the train. Now he was at Kennedy airport, waiting at the terminal exit, watching the shoals of yellow cabs gliding backwards and forwards.

A satin grey Cadillac drew up in front of him, its white wall tyres squeaking against the curb, and he watched the automatic window glide down.

Smiling at him from within was a face he had not expected to see.

The door opened and out stepped Francesca, her hair neatly combed down her back, wearing tight white trousers and a jacket that suited her, with a little make up, gold earrings. For a moment he hesitated, not sure whether she was friend or foe, then he saw Orsini in the obscurity of the car.

"You may kiss her," he said, "She's been working for me behind the scenes. Without her you would not be here."

She threw her arms around him, hugged him, clung to him, kissed his mouth, his nose, his ears, his forehead.

"Come on, get in the two of you," Orsini said. In silent luxury they cruised off through the flat landscape of Queens to the giant silver monoliths of Manhattan.

must understand is that you will be in a certain amount of danger."

"Why?"

"You are going to upset history, beliefs, everything the world has been brought up on. It's not a question of upsetting an apple cart, it is a question of you turning humanity inside out, and that will be dangerous for many, many people." Orsini stared at him all the way into Rome, like a child not believing his luck at Christmas.

"When Messalina brought you round last night I liked you enough already, but now!" He sighed. "The saddest thing is that I will never dare touch you!"

"We're here," Cadogan said over his shoulder.

And they got out of the van and went straight into the now familiar house where a woman secretary was waiting for them.

"They're suspecting something. Two of them are out front," she said as they went up in a service lift.

"Then we must get him out of Rome as quickly as possible."

CHAPTER
– 12 –

Orsini had made all the arrangements, elaborate and dramatic, as was his style. They had dyed his hair and smuggled him out of Rome on the train. Now he was at Kennedy airport, waiting at the terminal exit, watching the shoals of yellow cabs gliding backwards and forwards.

A satin grey Cadillac drew up in front of him, its white wall tyres squeaking against the curb, and he watched the automatic window glide down.

Smiling at him from within was a face he had not expected to see.

The door opened and out stepped Francesca, her hair neatly combed down her back, wearing tight white trousers and a jacket that suited her, with a little make up, gold earrings. For a moment he hesitated, not sure whether she was friend or foe, then he saw Orsini in the obscurity of the car.

"You may kiss her," he said, "She's been working for me behind the scenes. Without her you would not be here."

She threw her arms around him, hugged him, clung to him, kissed his mouth, his nose, his ears, his forehead.

"Come on, get in the two of you," Orsini said. In silent luxury they cruised off through the flat landscape of Queens to the giant silver monoliths of Manhattan.

He sat between Orsini and Francesca who held his hand tightly, studying him all the way.

"I didn't recognize you at first, do you know that? You look completely different."

"Better?"

"No. We must get you back to the sullen dark Latin American that you are."

Did she love him for himself or for what he was to become?

"You haven't asked why she's here?" Orsini commented, amused by his obvious bewilderment at the new set of circumstances.

"Why is she here?" Juan asked.

"I used her as a decoy. While the Vatican thought she was on their side, she was all the time on yours."

"As from which moment, though?" he asked.

"As from the time we were separated after the experiment with Sister Teresa. I was told to go. You didn't know that."

"How did you come to meet Signor Orsini?"

"I leaked the story of you going missing in the catacombs to the radio. *La Stampa* picked it up, and *L'Osservatore Romano* had to make a statement, by which time Cadogan had contacted me."

"Where is Cadogan?" Juan asked.

"At the Plaza where we're all staying."

"*The* Plaza?"

"The very same."

"I used to live quite near it," Juan said.

"Life does tend to go round in circles," Orsini observed.

The Orsini Organization had booked four adjoining suites on the eighteenth floor which were luxury plus.

In the cupboards of his room he was surprised to see a

whole wardrobe of new clothes his size, jeans, trousers, suits, shirts in abundance, shoes.

"Who did all this?"

"Janine, mainly," Francesca said. "Orsini's secretary."

"But how long have you been here?"

"One day. I left Rome twenty four hours after you did, but flew direct."

He took off his clothes shyly because he hadn't seen her for some time and was embarrassed. He then got into a deep foam bath she had run for him.

"Orsini has appointed me your social secretary. I hope you don't mind. This is the projected schedule."

She handed him a sheet of paper.

THE ORSINI ORGANIZATION INC.

Day 1. Arrival Kennedy.
   Book in Plaza.
   Press release conference (Not JRM)

Day 2. Press release.

Day 3. Demonstration to Press. (St Stephens)
   Cemetery mother.

He handed it back to her aware that he was pleased that everything was being done for him, aware too that he felt things might be going a little too fast.

He was allowing himself to be totally guided by Orsini, was taking no responsibility for himself at all. Eventually this might prove unwise, but right now he wanted to relax, wanted to enjoy the present.

Orsini came in to see that they were comfortable.

"All hell may well be let loose by tomorrow, so if you want to see New York you'd best do so between now and then. I'd like to introduce you to Catherine Katz, a nurse.

I'm having her on standby should any of us fall ill, also she is a walking encyclopedia on New York."

He left.

"Hi!" said Catherine coming into the bathroom to shake Juan's hand. She was in her thirties, an efficiently dressed lady with pencil eyebrows and long manicured nails.

Juan sank lower beneath the white bubbly surface of his bath, and tried to look as though he was used to such intimate introductions daily.

"What would you like to see first? The Met, the World Trade Centre or go shopping?" She was going to treat them like teenagers. It was going to be Coca Cola and ice cream time with a hamburger thrown in.

"I don't really care," Juan said. "I was born just across the Park from here, so let Francesca decide. I've seen it all."

He had no idea why but he was beginning to feel oppressed. New York should have been exciting, he had looked forward to it, but he felt that he was being bowled along now without being consulted first. Being given the star treatment made him feel uncomfortable. Was it that deep down he didn't want to make use of his powers, felt it might disturb the dead, and that this could have unpleasant repercussions?

"Demonstration to the press (St Stephens)." What did that mean? What if the dead started to erupt as his grandmother had done. What if they demanded release, the dead, demanded, demanded, demanded?

Who knew exactly what might be unleashed by the public declaration that he had knowledge of what went on after death? Maybe the church *was* right.

His dissatisfaction with the set up grew as the day passed. Francesca did not seem to be concerned about the project as a whole, not in the same way that he was. For her it was going to be like a party, like a first night, she would meet a number of important people.

He could not pinpoint the anxiety exactly, but he felt guilty at improving his lot materially by using powers he had been granted spiritually.

He stood by the bedroom window and looked out at Central Park. It was a park he had viewed many times as a little boy, rubbing his elbows on the window sills of his grandparents' apartment, bored out of his mind.

Who lived there now? Did his aunt and uncle, who had never written him and given him up for mad, still own it? They'd get a little shock the moment they heard he was back in town.

Maybe what Orsini had set up for him was against the law and he would be locked up with Francesca and everyone. He had to admit that he didn't like her quite as much now that she wore make-up. It made her look older and somehow false. He liked her in her plain cotton dress with the white collar, and that pale complexion. He could see her as an older woman now, rather plumpish with lots of jewels and airs that did not suit her.

They had dinner in the suite, Francesca, Catherine and himself. Then he said he wanted to go to bed. Ten o'clock it might be, but the jet lag and the journey had got the better of him and tomorrow was going to be a big day.

Francesca, disappointed, bid him goodnight, and he slipped himself naked into the huge comfortable bed.

He was exhausted really. Exhausted at the thought of what he had been through in the last few days, and exhausted at the thought of what might be in store.

Next morning, the day of the Press Demonstration, Orsini came in early to check that all was well. He was followed by Janine, Cadogan and Catherine who all came in to see if he was all right.

Francesca stayed with him to keep him company and calm his nerves, if he had any, but spent most of the time looking at herself in the mirror. She had chosen a simple blue dress for the occasion, which he preferred to the white trouser suit of the day before, but she still wore too much make up.

He had a bath, a long soak while a manservant he did not know laid out his clothes for him chosen by the great impresario himself. A white shirt, black tie, grey suit, black shoes, the uniform of the schoolboy, the innocent.

A barber came in to trim his hair and bring it back to its natural colour. He hated that. He had always hated having his hair cut. One of the great advantages of the monastery had been the once-every-two-months close shave.

The appointed hour came, they all went down in the elevator together.

Several reporters were hanging around at the entrance as he got into the waiting limousine with Orsini. A protocol had been established. He and Orsini in the first car, Francesca, Cadogan, Janine and Catherine in the second. The two cars moved off.

"Where are we going?" Juan asked. He had not been curious until now, had presumed it would be a cemetery next to a church or something equally undramatic.

"The church of St Stephens, on West 49th."

"A tomb inside?" he suggested.

"It's an old church I bought. It was a warehouse. I've had it cleaned up and carpeted and re-arranged so that it can seat three hundred people."

"Three hundred? All journalists?"

"All journalists."

"Television?"

"No. No visual coverage, in case nothing happens."

"How did you manage to drum up their interest?"

"My staff has been working on this for the past forty-eight hours non stop, Juan. I've invested quite a few thousand dollars in you."

"I'm sure you will be rewarded."

"I'm sure *we* will. One bright crematorium in Chicago has already asked if they can use your name."

"For what?"

"Promotion."

"But how has word got around what I do?"

Orsini dug into his pocket and brought out a piece of paper and an invitation card. A press release sketched in Juan's background and his experience with the dead and the near dead.

The invitation card was white, bordered with black.

ANASTASIO ORSINI requests the pleasure of..........'s company at the Church of St Stephen's, 2 West 49th Street, New York, on Tuesday 5th May 11 a.m. to meet JUAN RAMIREZ MONTONEROS who will attempt a psychic contact with the dead.

You are not asked to believe what you see or hear but you are requested to respect the silence necessary for the experiment.

RSVP

It was incredible.

"You've built me up like some pop idol."

"You want to talk to your mother, you want to find your father, this is the quickest way within the law. If all works, if you get through today and come up with the right answers, tonight the world will be yours, as I've said before."

The tone of near reproach told Juan to shut up and behave. He stretched his legs out and looked at his polished shoes, his grey silk socks. He had never worn silk before, he could see his skin through the thin material. He liked it. And the shirt was remarkably comfortable. He would wear silk for the rest of his life, and have a young Italian maid iron his shirts, a young girl, like Francesca had been.

They were driving through a seamier side of Manhattan: there were docks, warehouses, old unpainted buildings, faded hoardings, piles of garbage.

"O.K. now," Orsini said sitting up, "We're coming to it, so listen to me carefully."

He was keyed up, anxious, Juan had never expected to see him in this state.

"After you've gone through the preliminaries and your first enquiries with this body, you must ask one clear question and repeat the answer loudly."

Juan nodded.

"The question you ask is simply 'Where is your sister?' "

"Where is your sister?" Juan repeated.

"Right. Our future stands or falls by the reply, so shout it out as dramatically as you can. Remember that drama sells the big messages. If Jesus hadn't got nailed to the cross I doubt whether Christianity would have got off the ground. He gave the world a symbol based on drama. The masses need something like that to remember you by."

On West 49th Street there was a crowd half way down, police cars, a black and silver canopy, wreaths on the walls.

The crowd expectantly turned as they drove up, people peered in, looking at him, recognized Orsini who waved at them like royalty.

He was better known than Juan had realized, a cult figure, an impresario who manipulated the press, the business world and politicians like puppets, an international Machiavelli.

The car stopped, a man in black with a top hat, a funeral director, opened the door.

It was a pageant of death. Orsini had gone over the top. There were a few senseless cheers as he got out, a few cameramen who had been invited flashed away.

Juan walked up a black carpet, already white with dusty footprints, into the old church. Cadogan came up and took him through a door guarded by a strong man.

"Good luck," Francesca whispered, blowing him a kiss.

She was wearing high heels and a stupid white hat now, as though she were going to a wedding. He hated her for that, and for wishing him luck. He was not a performer with stage fright, he was going to communicate with the dead.

He would have to have patience and understanding, after all, Orsini had said, this was such new ground that no one could know how to behave. Once he had proved himself to the satisfaction of the world, then he could lay down the law.

Well he would lay down the law that the dead should be respected. They went down a side passage to the old vestry.

"Orsini wasn't sure whether you should go in holding a bible or not. It's up to you." Cadogan said. He was nervous.

"No," Juan said curtly. He went to the curtain draped over the door leading to the chancel. He could hear faint music, recognized Fauré's Requiem.

"Don't let yourself be seen, please," Cadogan begged him.

Juan peeped through the side of the curtain. Where the altar should have been spotlights shone down on a body covered with a white sheet laid out on a marble slab surrounded by flowers. Beyond the lights the church was packed.

Suddenly the spotlights dimmed and others came up brightly on the pulpit. Orsini climbed the steps slowly, tapped the microphone and wheezed into it.

"Ladies and Gentlemen, this is such a strange gathering for such a strange occasion that there is no traditional way of introducing you to the young man you have come to see. What will happen is unknown, and the body which rests there is at present unknown to you, its identity known only to myself and two other people. I do not expect you to believe me when I say that Juan Ramirez Montoneros has *no idea* who it is either, but I know you will appreciate that he cannot possibly know about the obvious secret the body's spirit could reveal, even if he had been working for the *National Enquirer*."

There was a ripple of laughter, for though Orsini's little speech was lightly delivered they were in a church and the sombre lighting demanded respect.

"There is no prestidigitation," he went on, "This is not a magic show. There will be no drama, no climax or anticlimax, the boy will put his head against the body's head, his questions will be heard through these speakers, but only he will hear the answers which he will repeat for your benefit. It is from these answers that you must deduce the validity of his claims."

There was a murmur of disapproval, two unclear remarks in scoffing tones, which Orsini ignored.

"Ladies and Gentlemen I will now ask Juan Ramirez Montoneros to join us."

Juan felt his stomach tighten. As the lights went up and he felt Cadogan push him forward, he got stage fright. He was out in front now, dazzled, nervous, very nervous, and he realized that this was exactly what Orsini had planned. Without rehearsals, without having been told what would happen, he was a complete genuine innocent.

He looked at the audience: hundreds of faces, women, men, all ages, papers in hand, pencils some of them, hard faces, smiling, sympathetic, disbelieving and bored faces.

Orsini looked at him. "Shall I take the shroud off?" he suggested gently.

"Yes . . . please." Nerves, nerves. His voice was so tight it came out high pitched and loud over the speakers.

For the first time he noticed a huge mirror hanging above the corpse at an angle so that the congregation could see it clearly.

Orsini pulled back the sheet from the face and there was such a gasp from the people that it sounded like a roar of the surf.

"Yes Ladies and Gentlemen, you are right. Do you know who it is Juan?"

"No," he said, truthfully, looking at the face, it was a young woman, early twenties, blonde, pretty.

"Geraldine Howarth. Does the name mean anything to you?"

"No."

"Nor the Coyote incident?"

"No."

Orsini turned to the congregation. "You are not asked to believe his ignorance, you are not asked to believe anything. He is however a boy who has been in seclusion in a monastery in Italy since he was fourteen."

Juan moved to stand behind the head and looked up at the mirror to see the hundreds of reflected faces. They would see exactly what he was doing.

He placed his forehead against the woman's brow and felt the ice coldness of it. He realized she must have been preserved in a deep freeze for quite some time.

Would it work, a frozen mind? He looked uncertainly at Orsini.

"Is something wrong?"

"I don't know. Has she been in the cold a long time?"

The innocent question brought another ripple of laughter which unnerved him.

"Don't worry, if you cannot get through, we have another person."

There were groans, unkind "ha-has," but they were going to get good copy from this whatever happened, so they gave him a chance, settled down as he placed his forehead against the cold brow again.

He waited for a long time. Long enough to become aware of a restlessness behind him, of a cramp starting in his left foot, of the tightness with which he was holding the marble slab with his hands, of the numbness the sheer ice cold of the woman's head was causing him.

Then he heard it. A long way off, but gathering speed. The hiss. The escape.

It came thundering towards him as he gripped the slab harder, it was loud now, very loud and stopped very suddenly.

"Are you there?" He heard his own voice echo through the microphones. There was a rustling sound now, a movement in his head, in the cavity, in the hall of death.

"What is your name?"

"Geraldine . . ."

"When did you die?"

"March 3rd . . ."

He started repeating every answer. "Where did you die?"

"My home, Burbank House, Washington."

"Where is your sister?"

There was a pause.

"I buried her in the Washington garden."

"You buried her in the Washington garden?" He heard a murmur of surprise behind him.

"Under the statue of Sappho at Burbanks."

"Under the statue of Sappho at Burbanks."

"Can you repeat that again," Orsini shouted.

Juan, rather abruptly disengaged himself from the cold forehead to face Orsini and the audience. As he did so he felt it was a mistake.

He realized instantly that this was what had happened with his grandmother when he had affectionately rubbed his head against her temple as she lay on her bed shortly after her death. He had not heard a hiss then, but a contact had been made and he had broken it, ignoring what he was doing. This is what had caused the fearfulness, the beckoning of the spirit and the abrupt disengagement.

It was a split second thought and he hesitated, not knowing whether he should go back.

"Will you repeat her answer," Orsini said urgently.

"She is buried in the Washington garden, under the statue of Sappho at Burbanks."

The audience rose to its feet.

Whatever this piece of news meant it was obviously an outstanding revelation, but he was not concerned with that, he was concerned with the body. He held up his hand.

"I'm sorry but I must have silence, I must re-engage."

As he turned to go back to the corpse it started moving. Imperceptibly at first, but a definite movement.

There was a scuffle, he was aware of people moving forwards. Someone shouted. "It's a plant! She's alive!"

Then the limbs started twitching, slowly the body raised itself to a sitting position, then in a frenzy of fearful vicious spasms it clawed at itself and started tearing out its hair by the roots then with supernatural force it dug its sharp nails deep into the rib cage, really deep, then hideously ripped out its lungs, its heart, its very entrails.

Paralysed with terror Orsini screamed out. "Stop it! Stop it Juan, for Christ's sake!"

Juan yelled at Cadogan. "Get hold of the skull, hold the head down!"

Cadogan, horror struck, moved towards the jack-knifed cadaver, the head and the trunk and the tearing waving arms. He reached out and got hit by one of the limbs, was knocked to the ground, covered with the spurting blood. Juan reached out, grabbed the hair, and the head like a rabid dog turned with foaming jaws and bit out at him, catching his wrist. Despite the pain he forced himself towards it, struck his forehead against the scalped bone and screamed, "STOP IT! I will help you! I will HELP YOU!"

The limbs convulsed, Juan was hurled against the wall, smeared with blood. Pandemonium and panic broke out in the church.

"Sever the head!" Orsini shouted.

Cadogan appeared again from nowhere with a fireman's axe.

Juan didn't want to see, but he got hold of the hair and swung the epileptic body round so that Cadogan could act. He saw him raise the axe, heard the wet crunch, felt the head come away, hurled it with full force at the wall. It smacked against it, slithered down leaving bloody slime all the way, and came to rest at the foot of the wall, its eyes staring wildly, a bloody, self mutilated hideous head.

"I have to release its mind," Juan said watching the trunk twitching on its own.

"How?" Cadogan asked.

"You have to disintegrate the skull, crush it, or burn it."

Cadogan handed him the axe.

Juan lifted it above his head and brought it down with all his strength on the head. It split open, like an Easter egg, the brains oozing out, flowing out. It was the sickest thing he had ever seen, had ever done, but as though hypnotized by the horror he impulsively stamped on it, like a fiend, like a demon, hitting the skull again and again, crushing the bones, mincing the slithering flesh till there was just a repulsive mass of splintered bones and sinews pulsating on the floor.

Cadogan came from the vestry with a petrol can, poured some gasoline on the mess, pushed Juan to one side, flicked a lighter and dropped it.

The fumes blew up in flames, there was an odious smell of scorching, black smoke belched out, Juan turned away, stared at the limbs which now stopped moving, the entrails which had stopped twitching.

The danger was over.

He turned to look at the people in the church. Several had passed out, the doors were wide open, there were policemen everywhere, blue lights flashing outside in the street and the continuous screams of ambulance sirens.

Orsini was sitting on the chancel steps his head covered in blood, maybe his own, maybe not.

Juan quite suddenly felt sick and was aware that his legs couldn't hold him. He sat down on the floor, which was sticky with mucous, but he didn't care. He wanted to faint, to lose consciousness and wake up somewhere else. He breathed in deeply, forced himself to sit up.

Cadogan was the stoic newsman, efficient, organizing. The church was emptied, the doors closed, a team of men in white from a hospital arrived to clear up the disaster. They came with plastic bags, rubber sheets, mops and stainless steel shovels.

Orsini was immovable. He refused to leave, and Juan wanted to stay with him.

"She must be incinerated," Juan said to one of the men in white.

"She already is."

"Totally," he insisted.

He watched the men clear up expertly: disinfectant sprays, powders, sand, everything was used, rapidly, efficiently, till nothing was left but a carbolic smell and a wet floor.

"Who was Geraldine Howarth?" Juan asked Orsini.

"Eleven months ago a very popular political figure by the name of Senator Edwin O'Neil was in line for an eventual Presidential nomination. It was certain he would get in. One night he reported that his wife was missing and the following day his yacht, the "Coyote," was found wrecked in Chesapeake Bay. There was no body, but plenty of evidence that his wife had been on board. Rumours started spreading, the press took it up, O'Neil was accused of having an affair with his wife's sister, Geraldine, and both were accused of murder. But it could not be proved. It ruined his political career and two weeks ago he took his life claiming that he was innocent. When she found the Senator dead, Geraldine also took her life, leaving the mystery open. That was Geraldine you were talking to . . . a perturbed spirit. I was able to borrow her body for several hours. I am owed a few favours."

Orsini put his heavy arm round Juan's shoulders and started leading him out.

In the vestry doorway they met Janine who barred their way. "They've found her," she said breathlessly.

"Who?" Orsini asked.

"Helen O'Neil, Geraldine's sister."

"Where?"

"Where Juan said. Buried in the Burbank garden, under the Sappho statue."

Orsini's expression changed from pained preoccupation to intense relief and wonderment. "Well you've not only saved us all from a lynching, Juan, but you've proved yourself a fairly extraordinary young man. I hope you'll be able to handle it all alone from now on because I have no intention of going through another experience like that again."

He took a number of deep breaths, and looked at his blood stained hands. "Let's get out of here."

CHAPTER
– 13 –

Juan awoke from a deep sleep induced by a massive dose of sleeping tablets to find himself in an unfamiliar bedroom.

It was bright with daylight and open windows gave out onto a clear blue sky. There were birds singing outside and the fresh morning air was quite beautiful. He got up to have a look.

He was on the first floor of an old house with a terrace below him and a garden extending down to a mass of trees. There were roofs beyond. He felt he was in a rich residential suburb.

He put on a bathrobe hanging behind the door, and went out into a carpeted corridor which led to a balcony overlooking a hallway.

Down in the hallway, lying on a sofa was Orsini, in a chair nearby was Cadogan in a neat executive suit. Between them was a pile of newspapers.

He started down the stairs feeling really well and surprisingly clear-headed.

Orsini looked up. "You are being described as a man of God, a Devil Incarnate and the Witness's long awaited Jehovah. It's like reading the bad notices of a brilliant opening on Broadway."

Juan looked down at the various headlines. O'NEIL CLEARED BY HOLY BOY, PSYCHIC WONDER CLEARS O'NEIL, COYOTE MYSTERY SOLVED BY TEENAGE MEDIUM.

Orsini picked up the *Catholic Times* and read. "Charlatanism in New York fools journalists. Anastasio Orsini, the Italian press mogul turned magician, stooped so low yesterday as to dismember a body in front of an audience."

He looked up, cleared his throat. "They'll fight you till they win, these people. I warn you. You'll have the Christian world against you and the rest for you. They will not believe and will not want others to believe."

"What happens next?" Juan asked.

"A legal enquiry. The Church of the Sacred Covenanters is going to sue you, bring an injunction against you accusing you of blasphemy, it'll be the trial of the century, of the millenium. With luck they'll crucify you and then you know what'll happen to your reputation for the next thousand years."

"Till then?" Juan asked, more interested in the immediate present than Orsini's future fantasies.

"Till then we hide you and collect the royalties from the articles which my team of writers are working on. Francesca is selling her life story worldwide, *Time* magazine and *Newsweek* will be granted interviews in due course. Film rights, television rights, television appearances, it's all in the pipeline. You've done more than split the atom and everyone is fighting to have a glimpse of you."

"I'd like some coffee," Juan said.

"Ring the bell."

Cadogan got up and pushed a bell button for him.

"Where's Francesca?" he asked. He hadn't seen her since entering the church yesterday.

"She is . . ."

Cadogan and Orsini exchanged glances. It was in their

eyes, something they did not want to tell him. She had left, had gone, frightened by what she had seen.

Orsini looked at more of the newspapers at his feet: British papers with sensational headlines. THREE KILLED IN NEW YORK PAGAN RITUAL. BLACK MASS KILLS FOUR.

She couldn't be dead.

"Two people were killed," Orsini said, "One badly injured, one is in a coma. Francesca."

"What happened?"

"The crush, the terror. The panic. She was struck down and trampled on, we think, but we don't know."

"Where is she?"

"In a clinic."

"Then I must go and see her."

"It would not be wise for a day or two. Here you are safe."

"I must see her. I will see her or else . . ."

"Or else what, young man?"

"Or else I'll stir up the power of the dead against you." He said it with a smile, but meant to threaten.

"Can you do that? Are you sure you can do that?"

"I'm sure I can make things uncomfortable for anyone who does not do what I wish."

"The two deaths are being considered by the police as homicide. The law wants you as well as the press. Do you think you can get your dead friends to help you against them?"

"What about my mother?" Juan asked, changing the subject.

"The Mayor is considering a request I have put in on your behalf. The request is for her disinterment. You are not God yet, Juan, the little people still wield a great deal of power."

Juan sat down and waited for his coffee. Things were beginning to go wrong and he didn't like it. *The Education of a Christian Prince* had never mentioned the press, the police or how to deal with the dead.

He was not a Christian Prince by any means. God knows what he was or what he was to become. Suddenly he felt drained.

Francesca in a coma? Like his mother. Would history repeat itself, would his father now show up like a vampire after an innocent white neck?

He did not want to follow that train of thought, but it was there, the coincidence, an ogreish Makar Boleslov raping his innocent Francesca.

He drank his coffee in silence then excused himself and went back up to his room. He got dressed in a white denim suit.

He could not analyze his feelings, but he did know that if Francesca died he would no longer belong to anyone. He had been annoyed with her, the irritation building up because of the tension, now he wanted to see her, wanted to see her in the coma, at peace, asleep, pale.

He went downstairs again and paused on the last step of the stairs. "I want to be taken to see Francesca." He did not say this as a request, but as a statement of fact.

Orsini looked at Cadogan. "Perhaps we had better do as we are told. Will you take care of it, using all your devious skills to avoid being seen?"

Because Cadogan chose to drive a small insignificant car and because no one knew where they were hiding in the first place, they got to the clinic on East 71st Street without trouble. Only a handful of reporters were hanging around the place and he went in by a back entrance without being seen.

Francesca was lying as white as a piece of marble on a hospital bed with one tube in her nose and another clipped to a vein in her arm. Her face was bruised, but the familiar peaceful expression was there.

Juan felt her pulse, trusting nobody, and bent down to kiss her gently on the lips. There was nothing he could do, she was obviously in the best of hands and could recover any moment. Or not.

When they got back to the suburban house without problems Orsini was anxiously waiting for him, having had an interesting conversation with the Mayor.

"I've made a deal. He will arrange for your mother to be disinterred by the corporation, if you will communicate with his mother too. She died a month back and happens to be buried in the same cemetery."

Juan shrugged his shoulders. He could see the shape of things to come. Already in people's minds he was being regarded as a specialist. They would call on him and for a fee expect him to communicate with a loved one: "My husband died last Thursday, could you ask him where he put the keys to the drinks cupboard?"

He would go along with it, this once, but never again after that. He was not going to be turned into a fairground act. He had started in the circus ring, from there he would progress, not regress.

A tent was put up in the middle of the cemetery and precautions were taken for total privacy. No one was to be with Juan when he made the contact with his mother, no one was to be allowed within a twenty yard radius of the tent. Orsini himself respected Juan's wishes and did not even accompany him. No one did. He was driven to the cemetery alone as dawn broke, was aware that photographers and journalists were around, but they did not make themselves obvious.

He entered the marquee. Two funeral directors were standing by in normal suits, no hats, no black, no pomp.

On a strong low table was the coffin, the wood swollen and cracked round the edges, rotted in one corner where water had seeped in. The lid was perfect, a good expensive mahogany coffin that had stood up well to seventeen years in the damp earth.

"We think you'll have difficulty in prizing the lid off sir. We have drills here, would you like us to do it for you?"

Though the men were very nervous of him they wanted to be involved with this boy who was making history, they wanted to have something to talk about afterwards.

"Yes please, go ahead. Nothing will happen." He was talking like a surgeon before an operation to the theatre staff, to the anaesthetists.

What was he going to see? Another skeleton, a partly decomposed body? After so much time, what would be left? He was unemotional about it. Would she even know who he was, would she even know what had happened to her once she was dead?

The two men in fact had no difficulty with the lid, the wood having rotted round the copper bolts. They lifted it off, bowed and left quickly.

Juan approached the coffin. The light in the tent was diffused, a peaceful light, there was silence, real silence, maybe in the distance the sounds of factory whistles, trains shunting, an aircraft somewhere, but distant.

He looked down into the coffin at the white silk shroud turned yellow and brown in patches. Carefully he picked up a corner and drew it back.

The face was only partly decomposed and it was hideous.

The dried skin had curled and stretched across the forehead, across the cheekbones like parchment, the lips, the ears, the chin had gone, and the bones of the skull were showing through. The teeth were clenched tight, there were gold fillings showing on either side. One tooth was quite white compared to the rest: a false porcelain tooth. The eye sockets were the worst, the eyes themselves like shrivelled eggs nestling in the hollows gave the face an odd gaze. Around the skull was a mass of brown hair, blonde in places, grey in others.

He pulled the sheet further back. Her hands were crossed over her chest. A rib cage of a chest now, with decomposed organs inside, not putrid but dry. Hanging loosely on one of the finger bones was a diamond ring. He slipped it off and put it on his own finger.

There was no smell, he would not need the cans of aerosol the directors had thoughtfully provided.

So this was his mother. In all honesty he could not feel any bond between himself and this corpse. He was doing this in the hope of finding out about his father, that is why he was here.

He bent down, placed his forehead in the usual position and waited for the tell-tale hiss.

It came eventually, slow as always, increasing in intensity.

"Mother?" he said. "I am your son, can you hear me?"

"Yes . . ." The voice was gentle, young.

"I am your son, I have come to release you."

"To release me from here?"

"Yes, from where you are."

"Thank you."

"Did you know you had a son?"

"Oh . . . yes . . ."

"It is I."

"I don't know what they called you . . ."

"Juan . . ."

"Juan. My name is Juanita."

"I know."

"Did my father look after you, your grandfather?" the voice asked.

"Yes. He died nine years after you."

"Nine years . . . ? And mother?"

"She died when I was twelve."

"It means so little, time. It means nothing. But it would be nice to go on . . . go on from here . . ."

"Mother, who is my father?"

"Your father . . . ?"

"Do you know who my father is?"

"Of course . . ."

"Did you know him before you died?"

There was a long pause, a long silence. For a moment he thought he had lost her.

He repeated the question again. "Did you know my father before you died?"

"Yes. A brief clandestine acquaintance. But I remember so little of life . . . I don't even remember how I died . . ."

"You were in an accident, a motor accident."

"Yes . . . I met him after that. He came to visit me in hospital."

"Where is he now?"

"How could I know . . . but . . . but . . ."

Juan was patient. He had learned to wait, knew that the thought processes were slow, slower in the long dead than in the recent dead.

"He left a message for you . . ." the voice said unbelievably.

"He left a message, for me?"

"Yes . . ."

He kept quiet. The mind was working hard at trying to remember, it hesitated once or twice, then came through, loud and clear like a pupil reciting homework memorized.

"The Octave born of the order of seven is seeded in the dormant womb. The Impulse sheds its life by fire before regaining awareness . . ."

Juan repeated it, twice, concentrating on every word, separating them into lines.

"Did he say it was specially for me?"

"For anyone who came to me . . ."

"Anything else . . . ?"

"Nothing . . . I am glad it is going to be over . . ."

"A question of hours, no more," Juan said reassuringly.

The background sounds faded. He waited a long time in the silence not wanting a repetition of the church horror, aware now that his body was numb, that he had pins and needles in his feet, that the back of his neck was stiff.

He waited, called out to her a few more times, then slowly straightened up lifting his forehead off her brow.

As he replaced the sheet over the skull and put the lid back on top of the coffin, as he wiped his forehead with a clean handkerchief, he repeated the message several times.

The Octave
born of the order of seven
is seeded in the dormant womb.
The Impulse
sheds its life by fire
before regaining awareness.

He called for the funeral directors and, exhausted, sat down in a canvas chair they had also provided.

The men took his mother's coffin away and returned shortly with another, far newer, a heavy set-man following, dressed in black: the Mayor of New York himself.

Juan stood up. A promise was a promise, a deal was a deal.

"She was embalmed," the Mayor said, shaking his head, "Died only five weeks ago."

The lid was removed. The covering sheet was crisp clean, the starch still stiff. Juan pulled it back. The face was like a waxwork mask on which cosmetics had been used like paint. It could have been the face of an old man, or an old woman.

"What do you want me to say to her?" Juan asked.

"I want her to know that I wish I could have done more and to thank her for making me out in the will."

"Did you have a secret between you? Something I wouldn't know about so that you can be sure it was her I contacted?"

"Oh sure . . . she used to have a nickname for me, no one would know that. I also would like to know how she became so wealthy without anyone suspecting."

Juan placed his head against the powdered brow and waited. He tried to clear his head, but had this image of himself doing what he was doing, like a doctor with a perfect bedside manner placing a handkerchief over the breasts of a female patient before pressing his ear to listen to her breathing. Commercially he could be very successful.

The hiss came, very faintly at first. "Are you there? Is anyone there?"

"Hallo? Who is that?" The voice was loud, abrupt, a voice that had been used to the telephone.

"I am a friend of your son."

"Are you dead as well?"

"No, but I can communicate with you."

"How is Pitsi?"

"He is well. He says he wishes to thank you for your generosity and also wishes that he could have done more for you."

There was a noise which could have been a grunt.

"He wants to know . . . he wants to know how you accumulated all your wealth."

"Gifts from rich men. Pitsi was always so naive, like his father. Gifts from rich men for services rendered. I was not always old. Once, I was beautiful. Tell him not to be shocked

and tell him to stop trying to reform the world. No good can come of that. Live and let live."

There was a definite silence.

"Is that all?" Juan asked.

"That's all."

"Do you want to stay where you are or be released?"

"If you can get me out of here, do so."

The definite void, the end, silence followed.

He waited a while, then sure that all was safe he disengaged himself, stepped back and nodded to the funeral men to replace the lid. He joined the Mayor out of their earshot. "She used to call you Pitsi," he said. "She made her money from other men, gifts from rich men. She said you were naive like your father and to stop trying to reform the world. Live and let live, she said."

The Mayor was stunned.

"A direct line to the dead, imagine that!" He thanked Juan with tears in his eyes.

"What about the cremation?"

"Yes, she would like that."

"I'll arrange it then. Your mother and my mother, together. Do you want to attend?"

"Not particularly."

He felt cold, not physically, but mentally, he was getting farther and farther away from reality and yet was not heading for anything else.

He did not expect crowds outside when he stepped out of the marquee with the Mayor, not this early in the morning, but they were there, thousands of them, silent, expectant, held back by a police cordon. When he was spotted an eerie murmur went up, followed by cheers and applause.

"Want a lift back with me now, son?" the Mayor asked. "I have outriders on standby which seem necessary."

"It might harm you politically to be seen with me," Juan

suggested, aware that Mayors were very susceptible to public images.

"The harm's done if there is any. Come on."

Heavy policemen closed in around them as they walked to the large city car.

"I've promised to appear on television this afternoon and talk about this," the Mayor explained, "Do you think 'Pitsi' is endearing or ridiculous?"

"The truth is never ridiculous," Juan said, maturely, after which conversation became impossible with the sound of the sirens, the hooting, the shouting and general pandemonium his very presence generated.

Cadogan drove him from Gracie Mansion, the Mayor's house, to the suburban hideaway in the middle of Forest Hills by such a devious route that they even lost their police escort.

Orsini was waiting for him. "So?" he asked.

"A riddle," Juan said, sitting down.

"A riddle?"

"The Octave born of the order of seven is seeded in the dormant womb. The Impulse sheds its life by fire before regaining awareness."

"Interesting," Orsini said. "We must think about that, meanwhile my theory that advertising pays has been proved right. This arrived for you at ten."

Orsini handed Juan an open white envelope inside which was a card. Written on the card in heavy black script was the name Makar Boleslov, and an address: 27a Mott Street.

"Cadogan will take you there tonight when it will be easier to avoid the press and your fans. The sooner you sort out your private problems the better. An announcement will have to be made soon as to the advice you are going to give regarding the after life. The world is waiting."

* * *

Mott Street was all Chinese restaurants and oriental bazaars. Number 27a was a small Buddhist temple behind a shop window, hardly bigger than an average hotel bedroom.

Juan, thinly disguised behind dark glasses and wearing a peaked blue denim cap to match his new blue denim suit, walked in and stared at the bald man in a kimono sitting cross-legged on the floor.

"I believe you can help me, I am looking for Makar Boleslov."

The man looked at him, studied him, then nodded. "You are the boy they have been talking about?"

"The papers . . . yes."

"Makar Boleslov, your father, is up there," the eyes indicated a casket on a shelf. Juan went to it, took it down, it was of black wood and carved on the lid was the nine-pointed star symbol.

"His ashes," the man said.

It was macabre. "When did he die?" Juan asked.

"On the day you were born."

"How?" Had both died? His mother and his father?

"He set himself alight on the roof of this building." The man studied him, studied his shocked reaction. "The Octave born of the order of seven is seeded in the dormant womb. The Impulse sheds its life by fire . . ."

"The Octave. What does it mean?" Juan asked.

"The first fundamental law of the universe is the law of three forces, the positive, the negative and the neutralizing. The next fundamental law of the universe is the law of octaves, the law of eight. Vibrations proceed in all directions, crossing one another, colliding, strengthening, weakening, arresting. Vibrations are believed to be continuous, but they are not. They need impulse, and when impulses stop the vibrations naturally stop. To us this is death. The impulses are based on the law of seven, like musical notes on a piano. Your father was one note, you another, and your son or daughter will be the impulse which will shock the world into revitalizing life vibrations."

"My son, or daughter?" Juan repeated.

"The Octave born of the order of seven is seeded in the dormant womb . . ."

He knew then what he had to do, and he would have to act now before returning to Orsini, who would block any attempt at such a criminal act.

He bid goodbye to the monk, paused a second outside the door of the tiny temple then dodged Cadogan easily enough.

Cadogan, an earnest hard-working journalist who knew when to keep out of people's way, was doing just that, sitting in the parked car facing away from the temple.

Juan, cap in hand, just walked into the passing crowd and took the first turning off. When he got to Lower Broadway, by zigzagging his way through Chinatown, he hailed a yellow cab and got into the oppressive passenger space behind the driver.

"The Columbus Clinic," he said, "39 East 71st Street."

There were several press photographers on the entrance steps, chatting, smoking, bored, so he told the driver to circle the block and look for a back entrance.

The driver found one, and Juan got out.

The door was open, there was no one in the goods checking office, he found some stairs and went up. On the ground floor he walked past the unoccupied reception desk and took the lift to the fourth floor meeting no one but an amiable smiling nurse on that landing. Room 404, he remembered.

No one was in the corridor, no one outside the door.

He went in, closed the door and turned the key. Private rooms in private clinics catered for privacy.

There was a shaded light turned so that the brightness

was reflected off the white wall. It was a tranquil atmosphere with no noise except for Francesca's very regular breathing and the slight tick of her heartbeat on the cardiac machine.

She had two tubes going into the veins of her right arm, and the electric impulse wires taped to her heart and her temples. Nothing else. She was lying flat on her back, a sheet and one light blanket covering her.

He drew them back and looked at her complete neat nudity. What was it that was so exciting about her?

The breasts? The triangle of dark pubic hair?

He stood over her, looking down at her breasts, not pert, not excited, yet the brown circles and the nipples stirred a feeling within him. He did not have to touch, just the sight of them excited. Was it because it had been forbidden him during his adolescence, or was it always so? Just nature?

The flat of her stomach, the dip between the hip bones, the navel. He looked at the curls between her legs. He had to touch.

Soft, yet tight. He stroked the hair, searched for that split, the warm softness which he had penetrated.

He moved his fingers looking at her face, wondering whether in her comotose state there would be a feeling, a reaction, but there was nothing. She was the near dead.

He however was not, and the feel of her, the touch of her provoked the desire and he started to undress. Within his trousers he felt himself getting bigger, his penis pressing against the zip, which he undid, slipping his jeans off. He was huge in his briefs, he took those off and looked down at his released manliness standing so firm.

He got onto the bed making sure he did not disturb the lifeblood tubes, checking the cardiac machine. He clambered over her legs, knelt between them, sat back on his heels holding her knees, his member well erect, and stared at her helpless body.

He now moved forward placing his hands on either side of her shoulders, then slowly lowered himself and up so that his tip touched her pubic hair and he tried to push himself inside her.

But she was tight and he was dry and there was resistance. He looked around the room. On the trolley shelf by the bed was a pot of ointment, a zinc and castor oil ointment presumably for bed sores. He opened it, dipped his fingers into it and covered his penis with it, then smoothed some into her.

He wiped his hands down the side of his legs, carefully put the lid back on the pot, replaced it on the trolley, and now, unable to contain his excitement, lowered himself on her again and eased himself into her, right up into her.

He closed his eyes, felt his bones against hers. He moved a little, felt himself deep, deep inside the warmth of her, felt his legs caress the smoothness of hers. He moved, forwards, backwards, very gently, the sensation was painfully delicious. He wanted to hold her, hug her, squeeze her, he wanted to be violent, but knew he must not. He moved more rapidly, deliberately building up the ecstacy then checking it, then allowing it again, till he knew that it would be a matter of seconds, a matter of split seconds, and he pressed himself forward as far as he could go and that slight movement released the flood, and he felt himself pumping life into her, felt himself being deliciously drained, and he remained there in her warmth as long as he could support his own weight over her, then he pulled away, pulled out and away and stared at the body he had so gently raped.

He went to the washbasin, washed and dried himself then with the damp towel he carefully cleaned her, remov ing the traces of ointment around her legs. Then he covered her with the sheet and the light blanket.

He folded the towel and put it on the rail, then he got dressed, and quietly unlocked the door.

It had been the seeding of one individual by another, nothing more, of the female by the male. Nature.

He checked all the tubes, the cardiac machine, nothing seemed disturbed. He then leaned down and kissed her gently on the lips and left the room. The corridor was empty. He walked down the stairs, feeling content.

A nurse was behind the reception desk. He smiled at her, she smiled back, it never occured to her what he might have just done. But he could not leave by the back way now, he had to behave normally and go out respectably.

Outside the reporters recognized him instantly.

"Juan Montoneros!"

They started taking pictures. They asked questions, he did not answer.

He hailed a cab and got away.

His picture took up the front page of nearly every newspaper.

The headline theme was HOLY BOY'S VIGIL WITH CHURCH HORROR VICTIM, and the stories either reported him as a saint or a sinner depending on the editor's stance on the subject.

Orsini, however, had no doubt which he was, and Juan watched him pace up and down in front of him, incensed.

"Why?" Orsini demanded, scratching his head as though about to tear out his hair.

"Compulsion," Juan said.

"What do you believe then, that your father burnt himself alive on the day of your birth to enter your tiny mind? Reincarnation, is that it? What are you going to do, wait till the child is born and then destroy yourself?"

"I don't think I am in control of my actions," Juan said.

"Who is, then?"

"The people that I was."

"The people that you were? You talk in riddles. Juan, there's a fanatical crowd out there waiting to hear religious pronouncements from you, and all you can do is talk in riddles."

"I think I am Makar Boleslov. I think I am his reincarnation, and I believe I must reproduce myself having achieved what was expected of me in this life."

"Expected of you by whom?"

"By the others who were me. By my previous incarnation, and possibly my future one."

There was a knock on the door and Orsini opened it to Janine. "His Emminence Cardinal Gregory is downstairs."

"Himself?"

"Yes, himself."

"Well they're not taking your actions lightly, that's for sure. What does he say he wants, Janine?"

"Just to see Juan, urgently."

"Get dressed then and meet us downstairs," Orsini said, and left the room.

Juan remained in bed for a moment longer. It was nine o'clock, a beautiful morning, he was still in the Forest Hills hiding place, undiscovered by the news hounds who were apparently searching for him much further afield.

Suburbs were deadly places for hunters.

So what did the Cardinal want? What olive branch of peace could he possibly hold out, and to what end? Had they decided to canonize him in the hope of bringing him back to Rome? He put on a dark blue silk shirt and his grey trousers and went downstairs.

The Cardinal's performance was unbelievable to the point of being frightening.

It was he who got up from his chair the moment Juan came down the stairs, and it was he who kneeled down before him to kiss his mother's diamond ring.

"Please get up, Your Emminence," Juan said, embarrassed.

"I have come as a matter of some urgency, Brother Juan. News of your miracle has reached His Holiness the Pope who wishes to see you before your trial, that is before you are examined publicly in the case brought against you by the Church of the Sacred Covenanters."

Juan looked at Orsini for advice.

Orsini had raised his eyebrows in surprise at the proposal, and was now obviously considering what would be the outcome of such a visit to Rome.

The Cardinal went on: "There is everything to be gained by accepting His Holiness's invitation, Brother Juan. Everything. The mere fact that you are being granted an audience can only confirm that the highest religious order is taking you seriously. We have, however, but one week. It was suggested that Brother Juan and whoever else he wishes should accompany me on my return, this Wednesday."

"Very good, Juan. I think you should accept."

"Then please convey to His Holiness," Juan said, "That I am pleased to accept."

For the next two days, while the Orsini Organization saw to it that the world media was informed about the Papal invitation and what it meant, while such magazines as *Time, Newsweek, L'Express, Der Spiegel* and *Now!* devoted their issues to Juan Ramirez Montonero's past, present and possible future, while debates went on in universities, religious enclaves on the radio, on television and in government circles as to the repercussions of Juan's contact with the dead, Juan himself stayed mainly in his bedroom in the Forest Hills house aware that his years of seclusion had accustomed him to the need of more peace than other people.

He wanted to contemplate his new position, wanted to meditate on the experiences he had been through, consider the demands that were going to be made of him.

Among the thousands of letters received from adulating believers and prejudiced bigots, sorted out into categories by Orsini's staff, one from his aunt in Buenos Aires unsettled him. It was a letter wishing him well in his "troubled" state and warning him of the dangers and evils he might come across in the "world of entertainment."

They had not understood, like millions would not understand, because change for them was impossible.

"It's all a matter of crystalization," Orsini said, "The majority of people get solidly set in their ways like reinforced concrete in their early twenties and nothing will, nothing can, alter this state. We, the more enlightened, jellify, then melt at the sniff of anything new, but most do not, unless they are given a massive shock."

So the system had sent him as a shock? As a first shock wave anyway. His seven forefathers had laid down the foundations for the launching pad, his father, in the shape of Makar Boleslov, had ignited the fuse, he had started on the trajectory and it would be his offspring who would cause the explosion. The eighth energy impulse, the Octave boost which would tilt world thought, which would melt the concrete minds. And all these men, all these generations, had been *him,* they were all one, planting their seeds in the near dead to re-incarnate physically, burning themselves to death to enter the mind of the being they had created.

He had to accept that this is how the system had willed

it, as he accepted without argument that amoebas and jelly fish and all kinds of plants had strange and wonderful births.

He hoped the Vatican accepted it, that they were not going to try to convince him that he was still mad and that all this was just the work of the devil. If they did, then it would mean a confrontation with the Pope and he would declare a verbal war until he had proved to all that what the dead told him was the undeniable truth.

They did not attempt to leave New York secretly, quite the contrary. They left in a blaze of publicity, Juan standing in the back of an open car next to the Cardinal, waving at the excited crowd, down Madison Avenue, up Fifth, over Queensboro Bridge and eventually to Kennedy Airport, a motorcade of the famous behind him, the Mayor, several Senators, thankful to him for clearing O'Neil's name, a film star or two jumping on the bandwagon and heads of religious orders wishing to align themselves with Rome.

After the plane took off and passengers were free to wander about, Juan decided to go to the washroom. He got out of his seat and started walking towards the back of the plane.

There were seventy-six journalists on board, sitting facing him and everyone of them, every face, was drawn, pale, grey and skull-like.

He knew instantly what it could mean, and felt very cold down the back of his neck.

He went into the washroom, the light came on automatically as he closed the door. He looked at his reflection in the mirror.

The skull stared back at him, charred and blackened, slowly confirming the premonition of his own death, of all their deaths. It lasted but a few seconds, but it was there.

He washed his trembling hands, aware that he was frightened, left the washroom and walked back down the length of the plane. Everyone was normal again: Orsini jovial, cigar smoking, Cadogan sipping a Coca Cola, the Cardinal, nervous, fingering his red leather executive case.

Was that it then? A simple explosive device? An assassination plot by the Vatican? His death in a plane crash over the Atlantic would rid the world of the threat he had become.

He sat down next to the Cardinal. "You are a brave man," he said.

"Oh yes, why?"

"Because in that case you have something which is going to kill us all."

The Cardinal twitched a smile and checked his watch.

"Yes . . ." he said.

The sheet of blue flame turned white, then vivid red, and Juan was aware of deafening sounds, of screams. He wanted to hold onto something as a hole opened up beneath him and he felt himself sucked into a vortex of intense heat, spinning round as he fell, seeing the ball of fire and melting metal which had been the plane disintegrate. He felt himself falling, spinning, circling, revolving and becoming smaller and smaller then settling in a comfortable darkness. He was cossetted in a liquid warmth where he knew he would be safe and secure, where he could grow, regaining his strength unharmed, where he could grow and be reborn again.

In the spring of the following year it became generally known that the young Italian girl who had befriended the Holy Boy of Death gave birth to a son, though she died shortly after.

In the Monastery of Monte Trasimeno, both the Abbot and Brother Ignatius felt a distinct shiver down their backs.

In a small Buddhist temple in Mott Street, a meditating monk smiled to himself.

And in every grave just below the surface of the earth, the dead stirred in hope.

"I have seen the future of horror... and its name is Clive Barker." —Stephen King

BOOKS BY *NEW YORK TIMES* BESTSELLING AUTHOR

CLIVE BARKER

___THE DAMNATION GAME 0-425-12793-1/$4.95

There are things worse than death. There are games so seductively evil, no gambler can resist. Joseph Whitehead dared to challenge the dark champion of life's ultimate game. Now he has hell to pay.

CLIVE BARKER'S BOOKS OF BLOOD

No collection of horror stories can compare to Clive Barker's gruesome spinechillers. "Clive Barker redefines the horror tale in his Books of Blood, bringing new beauty to ghastliness and new subtleties to terror." —*Locus*

___VOLUME ONE	0-425-08389-6/$4.50
___VOLUME TWO	0-425-08739-5/$4.50
___VOLUME THREE	0-425-09347-6/$4.50

Check book(s). Fill out coupon. Send to:

BERKLEY PUBLISHING GROUP
390 Murray Hill Pkwy., Dept. B
East Rutherford, NJ 07073

NAME_____
ADDRESS_____
CITY_____
STATE_____ZIP_____

PLEASE ALLOW 6 WEEKS FOR DELIVERY.
PRICES ARE SUBJECT TO CHANGE WITHOUT NOTICE.

POSTAGE AND HANDLING:
$1.00 for one book, 25¢ for each additional. Do not exceed $3.50.

BOOK TOTAL $____
POSTAGE & HANDLING $____
APPLICABLE SALES TAX $____
(CA, NJ, NY, PA)
TOTAL AMOUNT DUE $____

PAYABLE IN US FUNDS.
(No cash orders accepted.)

228